THE HOUSE SITTER

JE ROWNEY

LITTLE FOX
PUBLISHING

Also by JE Rowney

I Can't Sleep
The Woman in the Woods
Other People's Lives
The Book Swap
Gaslight

For further information and to receive a free
book, please visit the author's website

http://jerowney.com/about-je-rowney

ISBN: 9781739689940

ONE

Jude

Michelle Crane is one of the most recognisable women on social media and if everything goes to plan, I'm about to ruin her life.

I don't even post on my Instagram account, let alone have the millions, actual millions, of followers that she does. I'm under no illusions that I know who this woman actually is. The thing about identity is that it's a construct. It's just an idea. What is it that makes us who we are, and how can any of us prove that to someone else? I've heard her name. I've heard of her company, *Paper Crane*, and yes, I use their products. Who doesn't?

My diary, the one I use instead of the electronic calendar on my outdated smartphone, is a Paper Crane page-a-day. Over the three years since their ubiquitous stationery hit the shelves, I've bought their sleek notebooks, vintage ink coloured pens, cloud-shaped post-its and so much of that washi tape that I could wrap myself in it. If I wanted to. That brand logo, the origami bird, adorns most of the items on my cluttered desk. I, like most of the female adult population, am a Paper Crane junkie.

If you asked anyone what is so special about Crane's particular brand, I doubt they'd be able to put their finger on it. What makes Paper Crane so successful is the immense likability and relatability of Michelle herself. She's *almost* accessible.

Michelle Crane shares the minutiae of her daily existence on social media. She shares her hopes and dreams, and the millions of followers that hang onto her every post lap it up. They identify with her small-town-girl-makes-good struggle. Is that what she's really like, in what I'm going to refer to as 'real life'?

I'm about to find out.

TWO

I'm good at following directions, but I've never got the hang of listening to a sat nav. I've tried, believe me. It's just over an hour's drive from my small flat to Michelle's gated mansion in the hills outside of town, but the number of times I've ended up arguing with the ridiculous artificial voice is off the scale.

I've got it set to the rugged male Irish accent. Somehow, I thought he would be a better travel companion than snarky Jane or RP Richard, but I've still managed to find fault with my artificial friend.

What kind of lives must the people have who sit reading every combination of directions for a living? I wonder if they know how many people have yelled back at their calm, almost clear navigation. If I ever met smooth Dubliner Colin, I wonder if I'd recognise him from his voice alone. I imagine him to be a six-foot tall, rock solid, smooth operator. He's definitely got black hair with just the hint of a curl. I'm probably completely wrong. Perhaps he doesn't even sound like his narration in real life.

There's that phrase again. *Real life*. What does it even mean?

If I was concentrating more on my driving and less on my imaginary travel companion, or in fact if I was concentrating more on what he was saying to me, I might have realised that I was almost at my destination. As it is, I almost zoom past the gate that heads to the Crane residence. I slam on the brakes just in time, Colin repeating himself three times before I make the turn towards the entry.

"Shit," I mutter to myself, and instantly look around to make sure there's no one within earshot. The last thing I need is to blow it by sounding like a potty-mouthed loser rather than the sleek, professional house sitter that Michelle is expecting to interview.

There's a post, a metre away from the gate, and now, also, a metre away from the side window of my car. On that post is the intercom button I need to press for the gates to be opened for me. Because I made such a cack-handed job of positioning of the car, I can't reach it.

If Colin were actually here, I'm sure he would step out and deal with this for me, but his disembodied voice doesn't stretch to those kinds of skills.

I can back up and try again, or I can get out and take a couple of steps up to the intercom.

I'm already annoyed with myself, so I choose the latter.

I don't bother to pull the keys from the ignition. I slip the gear to neutral and leave the engine running as I huff my way out of the car.

My heels sink into the gravel, and I have to reach out, put my hand on the roof to steady myself. I hope she's not watching. I really hope she's not watching. I've got to make a good first impression if I want this job, and I want this job more than you can imagine. I need this job.

I press the squat little button that I couldn't reach from the car, expecting that I'll need to wait for a response, but immediately I hear a voice, clear and bold, from the speaker.

"Hello?"

I lean so that my mouth is in line with the intercom.

"Ms Crane? It's… I'm Jude Quinn. I'm here for the interview."

"I'll let Ms Crane know you're here. Drive through."

The solid metal gates swing open effortlessly, and I hop back behind the driving wheel of my boxy, outdated car.

I feel like a fraud, but I have every right to be here. This is my job; this is what I do. I get paid to bring my unique set of skills to those who need them.

If I'd managed to stop closer to the communication point, I wouldn't be wiping the grit off my shoes when I step out of my car and finally make it up to the door of the house. The last thing I want is to tread filth into what I expect is going to be a perfectly presented home. Despite not posting on my social media accounts, I've seen Michelle's photographs. Even if she wasn't a massive self-made celebrity, I get to view every property that's listed on the *Homesitters* site; I'd have seen the opulent overview anyway. There's no escape from other people's lives, especially when my job is to watch over what those other people hold most dear. With Michelle, I've done my research. I know what to expect from her home, but I don't know what to expect from my time here.

The front of the house is almost palatial, with two white columns on either side of the entrance. There's one small step up, cold grey stone, and my heels click-clack on it in an empty echo as I walk towards the door. Of course, the bell is linked to one of those video systems, and as I press it, I can't take my eyes off the tiny camera that I know is beaming my image inside the building.

There's a reason that people like Michelle Crane are internet famous and people like me are not. I can see my reflection in the glass panel over the lens that's peering at me, and I can't help brushing a stray strand of hair into place with my finger, and wishing I'd thought to reapply my lipstick before I got out of the car. I don't live my life in a state of social media readiness, but I hope I'm presentable enough to pull this off.

Just as I'm about to speak, the door parts in the middle, and I realise that there are actually two doors, so finely manufactured I mistook them for a single unit. Sleek, shiny perfection. I've never felt so out of place.

I step inside.

There's no sign of anyone else around, no trace of whoever answered when I buzzed from the gate.

"Come on through," a voice calls from a room somewhere to my right.

The floor in the atrium is polished marble, and I place my feet carefully, terrified that I'm going to misstep and slip. That's just the kind of thing I'd do: break my leg, mess up the interview before I even start. I watch every step I take, only looking up when I reach the doorway.

The woman sitting on the brown velvet sofa is unmistakably the entrepreneur behind *Paper Crane*: Michelle Andrea Crane. Michelle looks exactly like she does in all her social media posts. Apparently, it's not all filters and flattering camera angles; she really is that perfect.

Crane is dressed in a pale sand-coloured jumpsuit, just a shade lighter than her long, braided hair. Everything about her looks effortless and natural, even though I'm sure she must have spent hours ahead of our interview achieving her look. Everything is co-ordinated. Her outfit, her hair, the furniture. I almost feel as though I should have called ahead and asked for the dress code, made myself fit in with the colour-scheme. I'm making this place look a mess just by being here.

Michelle beams in my direction and, with a sweeping gesture, invites me to sit on a chocolate-coloured settee to her right. At least the muddy brown of my hair matches the décor. I can't say the same for my gravel-dusty black heels and navy skirt-cream blouse combo. I don't fit in, and I've already convinced myself that I'm never going to get the job.

"Good afternoon," Michelle says in a tone that makes me feel welcome and awed at the same time. "I'm Michelle, and it's lovely to meet you. There's a glass of water there for you, but if you'd like anything else…" She lets the invitation trail off, and I shake my head in reply. I could definitely use a shot of something stronger to give me a confidence boost, but then I'm sure I'd completely blow it.

"I know everything that you've shared on your page here," she says, gesturing to the screen in front of her. I can see from where I'm sitting that she has my Homesitters profile open. The strait-laced professional photograph I paid two hundred and fifty pounds for peers out at her, and I wish I felt even half as confident as I look in that image. Michelle is probably photographed hundreds of times a day, most of those images taken by herself. I had to spend an hour in a studio getting just one shot I thought was worthy of posting on my profile. And I'm not even completely happy with that one.

So much is riding on this position. I can't afford to make any mistakes.

Michelle carries on speaking. "Tell me about the real Judith Quinn," she commands.

"Jude," I say, without thinking. "It's just Jude Quinn." Never correct the client in the interview. Try to make a positive first impression. They are the employer.

I've already messed up.

A lump forms in my throat and I reach out for the glass of water.

"Sorry," Michelle smiles. "Jude. Tell me about the real Jude."

I nod and try to bring to mind the pre-prepared answer I had for this question, or one like it. '*Tell me about yourself*' is one of the most asked interview questions, so it's something I'm ready for. Or at least I was. My tongue feels too big for my mouth, and I've lost all ability to form words.

Remember what's at stake, I tell myself. *You need this. You need this.*

I take a breath, and ease into the moment.

Reeling off my spiel about how house-sitting is more than a job to me, it's a privilege. I can't judge what impact my words are having on Michelle. She maintains the same friendly, open expression throughout. I could have been telling her I enjoy collecting dead beetles in jars, and I'm sure she would have looked at me the same way.

Michelle makes encouraging sounds at the right times to get me through my prepared speech, and doesn't interrupt, not once. When I'm done, I search her face for any sign that might tell me whether I've made a good impression. I have no idea. Michelle Crane is so hard to read that I make a mental note to never agree to play poker with her.

"Wonderful," she says, and the mellifluous tone of that one word is enough to make me smile, despite my confusion.

Relaxing slightly back into my chair, I prepare for her next question, but none comes.

Instead, Michelle rises to her feet and offers me a hand.

"Let me show you around," she says.

Perhaps we are going to walk and talk. I'm ready for anything, but I'm already wishing that I'd worn flat shoes.

Michelle's hand is warm and dry, and I'm painfully aware of how clammy my own is. I wince at the thought, and imagine her pulling away, wiping her perfect palms on a monogrammed towel, then sending her servants to throw it in the incinerator. None of that happens, of course.

I try to fight back my nerves and follow Ms Crane as she starts to give me the guided tour.

The room in which we have been sitting takes up most of the lower floor. It's a vast open-plan area with cream walls and recessed arches set into one side.

Without opening the door, Michelle gestures to the first two inset entrances and dismisses them, saying, "Storage, more storage." At the third, she stops and pushes the handle down to reveal a room that is obviously her study.

"This is where the magic happens," she smiles.

The room is set into the corner of the house, and there are two walls with floor to ceiling windows, looking out into the garden beyond. To one side, the outlook is arboreal, the other gives a view over the perfectly landscaped stepped lawn and flower beds. I'd put my money on the fact that none of this was created by or is maintained by Michelle herself. Everything about this place stinks of wealth, but what a wonderful stench it is.

The office was not one of the rooms shown on the Homesitters website, so I'm actually genuinely intrigued to see where Michelle works. As I would have expected from seeing the living area, and from Michelle herself, it is impeccable. The large desk – probably three sizes larger than the one I have pushed against the wall in my tiny bedroom – takes up the centre of the room. Surprisingly, the surface is completely clear apart from her monitor and keyboard. There's not a single additional item on the desktop, not even a photograph. I have a momentary sad thought that perhaps Michelle doesn't have anyone close enough in her life to merit a place in a frame here, but I shake it away. She is one of the most popular women in the world; of course she has people.

The colour scheme is the same neutral palette, with a warm caramel vibe. The bookshelves, filled with a mixture of motivational non-fiction, are a formed from a pale wood that perfectly complements the décor. The same with the filing cabinets that line one wall. I can't help but think how relaxing it must be to work here. It almost makes me wish I had an office job again. Anyone could hack the nine to five if they had somewhere like this to work.

"I use my own products," she says, with a half-laugh in her voice, after she has watched me taking in the surroundings. She clicks a button beneath her desk and pulls open a drawer. Inside are spruced stacks of stationery, all with that recognisable origami bird logo. *Paper Crane.*

"This is…" I can't find the word to complete the sentence, but it seems I don't have to.

"Tidy office, tidy mind," she smiles, looking at me for a reaction. "Oh, that's all bullcrap," she says, actually breaking into a laugh this time. "I'm just completely anal about being able to find what I want. And I'm terribly easily distracted."

She swirls her finger in the air, implying that we should turn around, and I take in the room one more time before I comply.

Michelle strides on ahead, and I follow. She's not asking any more questions, and I can't help but wonder if this is all for show, that she just wants me to see what I could have won if I had answered the first question better, or had worn the right colour suit, or whatever I've done to dissuade her.

We walk through the open plan area and back to the atrium. The entrance hall is larger than my own living room, and a wide marble staircase dominates the space. Michelle pauses for a moment at the bottom and turns to make sure that I am still behind her. Her walk is confident and swift, and I've had to speed up my own pace to keep up with her. I'm not used to walking in anything other than flat shoes; these heels are strictly for interviews and date nights, and the latter are decidedly absent from my recent life. If I slip on these stairs, I'm going to be doing a lot more damage than the dent in my ego that it will create. I could probably break a leg, or worse. I try not to gulp and instead I give Michelle a broad smile as she leads the way up to the next floor.

I make it safely to the upper landing, where Michelle tells me that there are five bedrooms, all with en suites.

"This will be your room," Michelle says.

She's already talking as though she's offered me the job, but we seemed to have skipped that part.

I can't afford to make any assumptions.

To be certain, I have to ask her for confirmation. I smile, as warmly as I can, and clear my throat before speaking.

"Ms Crane. Do I… er, are you offering me the job?"

"But, of course," she laughs. "You wouldn't be here if you didn't have the job."

My mind works quickly. She doesn't mean upstairs in her home. She means I wouldn't be in her house at all. I swallow, trying not to show my embarrassment at my stupidity. I'd thought it was an interview, but apparently Michelle Crane had already decided before I even drove up to her house.

"Right, I'm sorry, I…"

Michelle shakes her head and gives me one of her social-media-famous smiles.

"Not at all. I should have been clear from the start. It's me that should apologise to you."

She appears so genuinely regretful that it makes me feel even worse about asking.

"Your profile is wonderful, and you're every bit as perfect in person as you are on paper. You're smart, self-deprecating, and sensitive."

Her alliterative run through of my qualities makes me blush, but hearing her words is an immense reassurance.

I've got it. I'm in.

So, this is my room.

It's hard not to imagine myself living here permanently, as Michelle shows me inside the storage space, the walk-in wardrobe and the deep drawers that would fit more clothes than I've ever owned. I'm going to be here for three days – two short nights – hardly enough time to even need to unpack, let alone utilise all the hanging space. As she waves her hand around the area, I can't help but wonder how often this room gets used, and by whom. She must have countless friends who come over to stay here for parties; I've seen the photographs of other blonde, slim trendcore sweethearts wrapping their arms around her, clinking glasses, raising drinks to the air. What would it be like to live Michelle Crane's life?

"I'm away quite frequently, I'm afraid," she says in a tone that conveys a genuine sense of apology. If I were her, I wouldn't be nearly so sorry to be travelling the world, no doubt first class all the way. "If everything works out this time, I hope you can come back again. It's so difficult to find the right person."

I'm about to reply when she walks past me, out of 'my' room, and back onto the landing. I can't help but feel relieved that I don't have to give a response.

We don't go into any of the other rooms on the upper floor, but before we make our way back downstairs, Michelle points towards a door at the far end of the landing, the room that must overlook the rear gardens.

"That's my room," she says. "I don't expect you will need anything from in there, and unless there's an emergency, I would prefer if you stayed out." The words come out bluntly, and she pauses after speaking and shakes her head almost imperceivably before smiling at me. "No offence intended, Judith."

"None taken," I say, not bothering to correct her on her use of my full name. If I need to go into her room, I will. If I must, I must.

"Good, good," she says, without pressing the issue further.

For a woman with so much to lose, she is remarkably trusting. My references are impeccable, and my police record is clean. Even so, I'm a stranger to her. If I were her, I don't know if I could be anywhere near as unguarded.

I steady myself with a hand on the rail as I follow Michelle back down the stairs.

Her voice rises from ahead of me. "So, I'll be away for three days. There will be a stocked larder. Everything you may need will be available to you. If there's anything specific that you would like me to provide…"

Michelle gestures, inviting me to respond, without turning to look at me.

"Thanks," I say. I'm concentrating on walking carefully downstairs, rather than focusing on the question. "I mean no, I'm sure I'll find everything I could possibly want here."

"I'm almost certain of it," she says, meeting me eye-to-eye as we both reach the hallway.

There's something so friendly about Michelle Crane's demeanour that I feel almost as if I am her equal, despite the ocean of difference between us. I'm on the edge of disappointment that she won't be at home while I'm staying in her house as a custodian. Even though we come from disparate worlds, I could see the two of us becoming friends.

I have to shake that idea from my head as quickly as it sneaked its way in. I am not Michelle Crane's friend, and I never will be.

Far from it, in fact.

By the time I leave this house, I will have done something that is going to destroy her reputation and bring everything she has worked for crashing down around her Louboutins.

THREE

When I'm not living in other people's houses, my home is a one-bedroom flat above a Chinese takeaway. The estate agent warned me that there would be a certain degree of *aroma* from the restaurant, and I assured him in return that it wasn't a problem. I needed somewhere to live at short notice, and I convinced myself that what I said was true. I love Chinese food, so why would the smell be an issue? Three weeks in, waking up to that same sweet sticky stench filtering through to every room in my flat and I'd already had enough of it.

I didn't always live like this. I used to have a regular job, and I suppose you could say a regular life. But circumstances change, and we have to adjust. Of all the things I've had to deal with, the smell of black bean sauce is one of the lesser evils.

The rent is cheap for the area, and I'm only in my own home for one or two weeks at a time, if business is good.

And it is.

You'd be surprised how many people from all kinds of walks of life hire house sitters. It's not just the Michelle Cranes of the world that pay people like me to look after their homes while they are away. A lot of my jobs involve glorified doggy day care, sharing clients' homes with their pooches while they're away on holiday.

I don't have pets of my own.

I don't have much at all, now.

What I do have, I'd go to any lengths to protect.

In the run up to my stay at Michelle Crane's residence, I've been at home for most of the week. The days are long when I'm not on assignment somewhere. I use that word – assignment – as though it relates to something a lot more glamorous or at least more intrigue-filled than a simple house-sitting allocation. This time, perhaps I am justified. I am on a mission.

I don't pack much for my stay. I'll be at the Crane residence for two nights, and I won't be going out anywhere during that time. Once I've committed to a house-sit, there's no space for social events, catching up with friends or seeing family. I'm in that house for the duration; that's what I'm being paid for.

I've gathered a functional wardrobe of comfortable clothes that I can fit into a travel bag. I take my iPad, phone, and earbuds and make sure I have the chargers. I pack my medication and make-up, and throw my toiletries in, although I've already noticed that the guest en suite has an ample selection for me to choose from.

Even when I'm staying in a luxurious location, I like to have my own little home comforts. I'm attached to my store brand shampoo and conditioner. No prestige label products can sway me from what I know and love. So much changes in my life that I feel a strange kind of reassurance from sticking to my own personal favourites. Three days away might not seem much, but things are going to change dramatically between when I leave this house and when I exit through Michelle's gates on Monday afternoon.

I'm almost ready to leave when, from within the depths of my bag, my phone starts to ring.

I curse beneath my breath and yank open the zip, hastily rifling through the contents.

Wasn't it one of the last things that I packed? It should be near the top.

Where the…?

My fingers close around my phone. I grab it and click answer, just in time.

"Hello?"

My voice is tense. I need to calm myself, and fast.

"Jude, my dear. I didn't catch you at a bad time, did I?"

"No," I snap, sharply. "I'm just leaving."

There's nothing but silence from the other end of the line.

"I have to go now," I say.

The line clicks: call ended.

I throw my phone back into my bag and tug on the zip to reseal it. I don't need interruptions; I need to focus.

Running through my mental checklist, I walk a circuit around the flat, making sure I've flicked all the switches off. I've not used the oven this week, but I check it anyway. Unlike Michelle Crane, I don't have the luxury of having a stranger staying in my home while I'm gone. If anything goes wrong while I'm away, it's on me. How ironic would that be?

I open the fridge to double check I haven't left anything that might spoil. The plastic bottles clatter in the door, but there's nothing that's going to go off. The shelves are almost bare; only a few jars remain from my weekly clear-out. Everything is in order, just as I knew it would be. The last thing I want is to be worrying about my own home when I'm staying in something else's.

I have to be organised. It's one skill I listed on my Homesitter profile: "An organised, reliable individual." I said it, so it must be true.

I lock the door and push down on the handle to make sure it's secure. There's no room to leave anything to chance. The one time I don't check will be the one time I make a mistake, I'm sure of that. Don't get me wrong, I'm not paranoid, I'm simply thorough. I should add that to my Homesitter profile too.

Satisfied, I throw my luggage strap up onto my shoulder and make my way downstairs, through the entrance at the back of the building, to where my car is parked and waiting. I don't bother opening the boot. My bag is small enough to sit on the passenger side, so I toss it there and settle into the driver's seat. Making sure I'm positioned correctly, I adjust the mirror, and check the car isn't in gear before I start the engine. Thorough, always thorough.

Even though I've already made the journey once, I set up the sat nav again. If there are any delays, Colin will amend the route. I want to make the best use of my time, and I definitely don't want to be late. I said I'm organised, and I mean it. I don't want to give Michelle any reason to doubt that I'm true to my word.

Finally, I'm ready to make the hour-long journey out of town.

Things are about to change, for Michelle, and for me.

FOUR

When I pull up outside the gate to Michelle Crane's house for the second time, I don't make the same mistake. I judge the distance perfectly and as my window opens, the intercom button is exactly aligned with where I need it to be. I reach out and press once.

This time there's a slight pause before the answer comes.

"Ms Quinn? Drive through."

No need for my response. There's a gentle whirring sound and the gates open to let me inside. Everything is so much smoother today, and I can't help but take this as a good omen.

I drive up to the front of the house and pull into same the parking space that I used only a few days ago. Today I'm wearing flat pumps, a plain navy midi dress and a cropped cardigan I threw on just in case. I don't need it. The sky is bright, and it's shaping up to be a perfect spring day.

Before I even reach the front entrance, I see the doors open. I'm not expecting to be letting anyone into the house, but I make a mental note to ask how the remote mechanism works.

It's minor details like that, and my attention to them, that lands me jobs like this. I'm not one to sing my own praises, but I'm good at what I do. I know I'm one of the best.

"Jude, I'm in the kitchen. Come through."

I wouldn't have pegged Michelle for someone who has to prep food for herself, but there she is, as I walk into the airy, high-ceilinged room, wrapping foil around some kind of sandwich.

"Even in first class, I never seem to be able to get a sandwich that compares to the ones I can make for myself," she smiles, patting the top of her foiled package. "Corned beef and tomato with a smear of mayonnaise." She cocks her head, and with an apologetic tone she says, "I should have made one for you. I'm sorry."

"No. Not at all," I laugh. "Sounds great, though."

"There are plenty of extra supplies," she says, tapping the fridge door. "Make sure you try one for yourself."

Even dressed for her flight in loose-fitting coffee-coloured pants and a thin cocoa suede jacket, Michelle Crane is stunning. I wouldn't be surprised if she held a mini photoshoot for her lunch making and pre-flight prep. Everything in her life appears to be a shareable event. If my life were as perfect as hers, maybe I would want to share it with 12.5 million followers too.

But my life is nothing like hers.

"Thanks," I smile.

Michelle slides her lunch package into a monogram-print tote bag and slings it up onto her shoulder.

"I'm afraid we are going to be leaving you now," Michelle says. Before I have time to wonder who the 'we' refers to, a young, slim blonde woman comes walking in from the hallway.

She's decidedly average looking, and even though she is dressed in clothes that appear expensive and stylish, she doesn't pull the look off in the way that Michelle does. Her presence only serves to further magnify Michelle's style.

I don't know whether to say hello, seeing as it looks as though we are about to say goodbye. Instead, I end up staring at the woman like a rabbit in the headlights. I instantly feel my stupidity causing a flush in my cheeks and look away.

"This is Hester," Michelle says, waving in the woman's direction. "She's my…" Michelle pauses and looks at Hester. "I suppose Hester could best be described as my PA. She helps me to plan and organise everything that I need to, er, plan and organise. She's my angel, she really is. But unfortunately, Hester has a home and a family of her own, and won't give them up to come and live here with me. She's even threatening to go part-time on me."

There's something in her voice, an edge that I can't quite put my finger on. Whatever it is, there's some deeper meaning to what she is telling me, some backstory that she isn't going to come out and reveal to a near stranger, that's for sure. I decide to let it go. I don't need to know the details about Michelle's life, or at least not when it comes to Hester. She won't be here, and that's all I need to know.

Hester doesn't smile; she looks me over with a cool expression, and then turns her gaze to Michelle.

"Are you ready?" she says.

"Personal organiser, perhaps." Michelle shows off the expensive dental work beam that I'm sure she could trademark, and this time, Hester casts a small, slight upturn of her lips in Michelle's direction.

I thought I might have had time with Michelle before she left, to go over security arrangements and whatever else she feels necessary to tell me, but she already looks anxious to leave.

As an afterthought, still seemingly trying to explain the other woman's presence, Michelle rests her hand on Hester's arm and addresses me.

"This girl is my angel. She really is. I wouldn't be anywhere without her."

Hester flicks her eyes in my direction, and I almost think she is going to speak, but instead she rolls her eyes at Michelle and huffs out a slight laugh.

"Let's go," Michelle says, and raises her hand like a signal. "I want to get a couple of cocktails in at the lounge before the flight. I know you won't believe it," she leans in to whisper to me conspiratorially, "but I actually hate flying."

All those photographs of her showing that expensive smile in airports, on planes with those little oval windows showing clear blue beyond, they must have all been lies. But then again, how much of what people do for social media is real, and how much is put on to impress other people? Michelle Crane has a lot of other people to impress. For now.

"Ready?" Hester asks.

I wonder if the harsh edge in her voice is somehow related to my presence here. I try to shake off the thought as guilt-tinged paranoia.

I flick a look in her direction and although Hester is talking to Michelle, she is staring at me. Her eyes are such a dark brown that they are near ebony, and that, along with the death glare she's aiming my way, is enough to make me avert my gaze again. She will be gone soon. Both she and Michelle are going to be out of here and out of my way so that I can get on with my job.

"Have I got everything?" Michelle says, as she looks around the room. It feels like a rhetorical question, and Hester obviously takes it as such because she doesn't give an answer. Instead, she walks out into the hallway, where the influencer's bags are waiting.

Hester scoops Michelle's travel bag onto her shoulder and takes the handle of her trolley case. The amount of luggage Michelle has for her trip compared to what I have brought with me for the same length of time is striking.

As Michelle makes to follow Hester, she stops in front of me. I reach out my hand to shake with hers, and she leans forwards instead, wrapping me in an over-friendly hug. It takes me by surprise, and my breath hitches in my throat.

Michelle smells exactly how she looks: expensive and sophisticated. Whatever shampoo she uses has given her hair a warm, creamy scent that's somewhere between floral and edible. It's impossible to describe, but I want to keep my face pressed into it, inhaling that delicious aroma. I have to snap myself out of the daydream and politely pull back.

"Have a great trip," I say, trying to maintain professional etiquette.

"You have my numbers," Michelle smiles. "If you need anything at all, please don't hesitate to get in touch."

"The security system is still up and running, I assume?" I try to make the question seem like an innocent enquiry. It's the sort of thing that homeowners usually tell me about without needing to be asked.

"*You* are the security system, sweetheart," Michelle laughs. Having a thirty-year-old woman call me 'sweetheart' sounds very strange, but so does referring to me as the security system. Still, I release an internal sigh of relief and laugh along.

Your secrets are safe with me.

I almost say it but stop myself just in time. Her secrets are secret. As a hired professional, I should have no way of knowing that she has any skeletons in her closet, let alone be plotting how I can excavate them.

Hester is already lumping Michelle's luggage out to the four-wheel drive that's parked beside my tiny hatchback. Looks like I don't get to share an awkward hug with her.

I'd assumed that Michelle would have her own personal driver, or at least would have called a car to take her to the airport. If the pair of them are taking the trip together, I suppose it makes sense for Hester to drive. Airport parking isn't cheap, but Michelle Crane isn't short of money. I doubt it would be a consideration for her.

Michelle introduced Hester as her PA, but it appears that her role extends far beyond that. I can't help but think that there's something that I don't know. Perhaps it covers everything except watching Michelle's home while she is away. As long as she will not be here while I am, that's all that matters.

Having someone else in the house certainly wasn't in my plan. If Hester hung around, it could ruin everything.

Michelle steps through her doorway, out into the early summer sunshine, and the light makes her hair glow like spun gold. I'm almost tempted to take out my phone and take a photo of this Instagrammable moment for her. It's just the kind of thing her followers would lap up. Every step she takes seems to create more photo opportunities. It's no wonder she's such a popular figure.

"Have fun, Jude," Michelle calls over, as she climbs into the waiting car.

She raises her hand from the other side of the closed door, and I give her an awkward wave in return.

"Bye," I mouth, as Hester drives them away down the gravel driveway.

Michelle has left her property in my more than capable hands. As the car pulls out of sight, I can't help but wonder what she would think if she knew the real reason that I was in her beautiful home.

FIVE

Libby

It's dead on three o'clock, and I'm ready. I've spent the last two hours going over my slides, making sure every detail is meticulously planned, all the data is watertight, and that I'm ready to answer anything they throw at me.

"The committee is ready for you, Miss Halstead."

The voice from the doorway is clear, but all my focus is on what I am about to do. This presentation needs to be perfect, and it looks like it's time to deliver.

"Miss Halstead?"

It's Mrs Halstead, but I don't correct her. I've been contracting at this site for six months now, and it seems too late to start worrying about such trivialities. Nobody knows me, but that's because I haven't given them the opportunity. Today I am here, and next week I will be gone. That's exactly how I like it.

I look over and give her a thumbs up. The woman smiles in return and nods, scurrying off to the conference room to take her seat.

This is the moment I've been working towards. Finally, after half a year of planning, today the wheels will be put in motion. It's launch day.

No matter how many times I've been through this, how many different projects I've headed, how many presentations I've given in how many companies, I'm never confident until the gears click into action, and I see the results of my hard work.

I scoop up my laptop and paperwork and go through to the room full of people who are waiting to see what I have produced for them.

Sawyer Braun is one of the most important HR companies in the south of England, and I'm responsible for rolling out the project that's going to keep their three thousand five hundred and seventy-two staff working. I have a head for figures. If I make the slightest mistake, you can guarantee that someone will pounce on it. A miscalculation or a decimal point sitting out of place could lead to the entire development falling apart.

I haven't opened my notebook. It's a prop, not a prompt. I don't need to flip open the cover of my A4 planner to remember what to say.

I take a sip from the glass of water and slowly rise to my feet.

It's showtime.

When I finally stop talking, the director starts to clap her hands, and the rest of the room follow suit. The validation of my hard work is imminent but I'm ready to step out of the limelight. I've done my job, that's all. I don't need the standing ovation they're giving me. Still, I adopt my standard professional smile and try to stop myself from blushing.

"Thank you. Thanks so much," I say, bowing slightly, unsure what the appropriate response is to this kind of adulation.

I stand, shuffling slightly as the sound in the room dissipates, and the director makes her way to join me.

"Very impressive," she says, in a low tone, before addressing the twenty-three committee members, who are smiling up from the seats before us.

"I'm sure you can all agree," she says in a calm, confident tone, "That this is the solution we have been looking for. Miss…Mrs Halstead has identified a pathway that I am more than happy to support."

She turns to me again, still glowing with the knowledge that what I have proposed for them is going to help their company to save a vast amount of money and no doubt countless jobs. I worked hard. I did what they asked me. I'm ready to go home.

I can see from the clock on the wall at the side of the room that it's already past five pm. I should have finished earlier. I should have opened for questions at the end instead of answering them as I went along. I thought I had time, though. I was foolish, and despite the applause and the words from the director, I can't quite feel as happy as she does. I need to leave.

"Thank you," I say again, trying to draw the meeting to a close. I've given my presentation. I've met their expectations. I need to leave.

Either the director has seen me looking at the clock, or she has sensed my discomfort, as she smiles, and seems to back down.

"Let's not waste any more of Mrs Halstead's time," the director smiles towards the room. "We'll reconvene at nine tomorrow and iron out the next steps."

There's a muffled murmur of assent throughout the committee members, who are probably also happy to leave. I fear for a moment that she is about to lead another ovation, but instead she shakes my hand.

"Brilliant," she beams, as the room begins to empty. "Listen, did you want to go and grab a celebratory glass of wine or something? On me, of course. I don't have to be anywhere just yet, and you've definitely earned it."

I do have to be somewhere. I have to be somewhere very soon.

"I'm so sorry," I say as politely as I can manage. "I have plans this evening."

"Another time, then," she smiles, giving me a look that could only be described as bemused, as though she has never been turned down for free drinks before.

I nod in false enthusiasm and return the smile.

The director steps away and nods.

"Don't let me keep you any longer then. And again, thank you."

I can't keep finding new ways to accept her gratitude, and I can feel my anxiety rising at how quickly the minute hand on the clock appears to be moving. I gather my papers together and open my tote to slide them inside. Despite everyone's enthusiasm, all I can think about is getting out of here and making my way home.

I make it as far as the corridor before one of the committee members taps me on the shoulder.

My tote is heavy, and my time is short. Still, I do the polite thing and pause, turning to find out who is trying to get my attention.

The grinning face of one of the office guys, a kind-of-handsome-if-that's-what-you're-into type called Eduardo Mendez, greets me. I'm sure that whatever he wants to say to me he could have managed to speak out in front of everyone else. I grit my teeth and return the smile.

"That was great," Eduardo says. "You've done an amazing job."

In fairness, he doesn't know if my work has been amazing. I made a good presentation, but the proof of the pudding is in the eating, or in this case the proof of product is in whether it works as planned. We'll find out over the next few days whether there are any unforeseen glitches. I'm fairly confident, though, that there will be none.

"Thanks," I tell him, hitching my bag into a more comfortable position on my shoulder. The word has started to lose meaning for me, I've said it so many times.

The day has already run over. The clock tells me I'm now twelve minutes behind schedule, and I know what that means. I have to be on my way home, and soon.

"Listen, I was wondering if you would like to…"

I already know where he's going with his sentence, and I cut him short. What is it with these HR types and their need to turn everything into an excuse for a social event?

"I'm so sorry," I say, although I'm really not. "But I have to get going. My husband…" I let the words trail off, hoping that I've said enough.

"Right. Of course," he says. "Well, maybe another time."

Another time, another time. Nobody can take a refusal as an absolute.

There won't be another time. There's no chance that I will ever go to wherever Eduardo is inviting me, no matter where it is. He seems like a decent guy, and the band on his finger tells me that he's no doubt a family man too. It doesn't make a difference. I don't socialise outside of work hours, not with anyone.

"Sure," I lie. "Sounds great."

And with that he lets me turn towards the door before reaching around me awkwardly to hold it open while I walk through.

It's twenty past five by the time I slide behind the leather-bound steering wheel of my Tesla. When I check my mirror, the face that looks back at me bears an expression that's a mix of exhaustion and anxiety. It's been a long week, let alone day. I should be feeling the elation of completing the project and delivering on time, but instead I wish I was already home.

I don't have time to sit outside the office feeling sorry for myself. I need to get moving before I make myself any later. It's a half hour drive across town and at this time of the day there's no way that I can make up any of the lost time. The traffic is likely to be chock-a. If

I'm really unlucky, I might get caught up and held back even further. I need to get moving. I've got to get home.

When I pull up to the house, the light in the lounge is glowing between the chink in the curtains. I don't know how long he's been standing there, waiting for me to get home, but when he sees me, he steps away, back into the room.

What I should do is start the engine back up, drive away and never return.

But it's not that easy.

My whole life is in that house. Everything I own. Everything I've worked for. Everything I've built with him. Leaving him means leaving all of that, and without that, who am I?

I'm one of the leading experts in my field, that's who I am. I'm a postgraduate specialist, headhunted by every major corporation that needs my skills, an award winner several times over. I've implemented new systems that have saved time and money for national and international organisations.

And I'm afraid to walk in the front door of my own home.

SIX

Jude

My room in Michelle Crane's mansion is far nicer than the one I have in my tiny apartment. In fact, it's nicer than any room that I have ever stayed in before. Whoever Michelle's interior designer is – and I could probably find that out by scrolling back through her Instagram posts and seeing who she tagged – they've put just as much effort into this barely used king-sized guest room as they have with the rest of the house. It's neutral but opulent. The walls are painted in a satin-sheen finish that gives me the feeling that I'm being wrapped up and drawn in.

I only have a single holdall bag, because I've trained myself to travel light, but it seems like such an inadequate amount of clothing for the huge armoire that sits opposite the sprawling bed. As there's a walk-in wardrobe tucked away too, I know the armoire is just for show: an extravagance that probably cost Michelle more than I earn in a year. Maybe I'll unpack later when I'm alone in the house and need something to do to occupy myself.

I need to start working on the task in hand. Before I start though, I pause and pat the deep down duvet. My hand sinks into the covers and I can't stop myself from flinging my body into the middle of the bed.

Let me enjoy this moment.

I have three days, just three days. It sounded like plenty of time, but lying here, letting the luxurious surroundings envelope me, I wonder. Perhaps it won't be enough. I would love to be able to enjoy this feeling, the buzz of living a life that isn't my own, but I have a job to do. If I fail, the consequences are going to be unimaginable.

There's no time for this, none at all. Not just the lounging around enjoying my stay, there's no time to feel comfortable here. I need to get to work.

I press my hands down into the soft cloud of bedding and bring myself up to a sitting position. I can see my reflection in a full-length mirror on a stand, by the armoire, and I'm surprised at how small I look. I haven't shrunk, but my surroundings are so much bigger than I am, this life that Michelle lives is so much bigger than mine.

I feel like Alice in Wonderland after she bites the cookie, or whatever it was, that says 'Eat Me'.

I feel like an intruder.

I feel like a fraud.

And I am.

Unable to look at myself any longer, I push up off the bed, and pad across the thick cream carpet into the bathroom.

The en suite isn't just a flimsy add-on to the guest bedroom, it's the size and standard of a main bathroom, including the actual bath itself. Everything is cream marble, and the shower is one of those amazing waterfall types that I've only ever used in other people's homes. I've house-sat for some impressive clients in the past, but none have come close to the magnificence of Michelle Crane.

I run my hand along the smooth surface alongside the sink, and despite the marble, it feels warm to my touch, as though everything has been heated to the ideal, palatable temperature. Michelle has spared no expense, and I know that under other circumstances I would have an amazing relaxing break during my placement here. Instead, though, I have a gut-thudding feeling of guilt before the act. I know what is coming. I know what I have to do while I'm here.

Three days.

Three days may seem like a long time, but in reality, it's just a blink of an eye. I know I have to work tirelessly, without rest or pause, if I want to succeed. The pressure is immense, but I have no choice but to rise to the challenge or face the dire consequences that await me. Once I've done what I came here for, maybe then I can relax and enjoy the house; do what on paper is my real job. When I've got what I came for, I'm not just going to up and leave. I'm too much of a professional for that.

My reflection is looking out at me again, this time from the bathroom mirror, this time in the kind of close proximity that reflects my every imperfection and flaw. This is the person who Michelle saw. This is who she let into her house to guard everything that is precious to her. This is the person who is going to betray her.

I stare dead into my own eyes and wonder how it came to this.

I'm near hypnotised by my own soul-searching stare when a ringing from the bedroom snaps my focus back and makes me spring forward, so I knock my knee against the sink cupboard.

"Motherf…" I yell before stopping myself. There's no one to hear me cursing even if I finish the word.

The jolt through my patella is overwhelmingly painful and I get a heavy sickening lurch in my gut and have to steady myself.

The phone continues to ring.

"*Just let me get on with it*," I mutter to myself in a voice I barely recognise. My words are hard and dry. Every minute I'm veering further away from the person I really am, and becoming a version of Jude Quinn that I can't help but hate.

Rubbing at my knee as I hobble through to the bedroom, I spot my bag on the dressing table, and thrust my hand in for the phone.

"Jude, my dear."

Always the same. It's almost as though my unwanted caller knows how much this greeting irritates me. They don't care. Why would they?

"I'm here," I say, flatly, trying to hide my emotions. I won't let them get inside my head. I can't give them any more power over me.

"Perfect," the voice almost purrs.

"What do you want?" The pain in my knee is making it difficult for me to keep my voice steady, but I do my best.

"You know what I want." Every word is loaded with a vicious edge.

"I'm…"

Before I can say anything else, the line falls silent, dead.

The tiny figure in the full-length mirror looks at me, and I turn away.

I have to do this. There's no alternative. There's too much at stake.

I have to do this, and I have to start now.

SEVEN

As Michelle so succinctly stated, I am the security system. The outside of the Crane residence may well be monitored by cameras, but inside the house, the doors are lock-free and there's no video surveillance. I can wander around as I please. I could sit on the lush leather sofa in my pants for my entire stay if I wanted, and no one would be any the wiser.

I don't intend to do that, of course, but whatever I choose, there will be nobody to see me.

Always prepared, I had plans for what I would do if the house *was* monitored. A power outage, triggered by some foolish mistake, disabling the system for just long enough for me to do what I need to do. I'll never know if that was going to work, because thankfully I'll never need to find out. My track record at Homesitters and my glowing references have given me the credibility I need to carry this off.

That's why it's me, here in Crane's mansion.

That's why I am the one who must do this.

The throbbing pain in my knee has dissipated, but I take it easy as I walk back down the stairs. I'm not making the mistake of wearing heels in this house again, but now I have no need to. My work wear is casual and comfortable; after all, I'm supposedly simply sitting around a house for three days.

I hold on to the banister as I walk, treading carefully, but feeling a strange sense of majesty as I descend the decadent stairway. It's like walking into someone else's dream. The luxury and style almost make me want to start taking photographs to capture my surroundings too. All of this has been carefully designed to look aesthetically stunning, and whoever did it was bang on the money. Literally.

The house seems even larger with only me here. Not that Michelle takes up a lot of physical space, but there's something about her presence that fills a room. Maybe it's simply that when she is around, she is the only thing I can look at. That makes it sound as though I am terribly star struck, but I'm not. It's her. There's something about Crane, and there's no getting away from that.

I wonder if that is going to change once I complete my mission.

I have to shake that thought away. I'm not going to derive any pleasure from what I am about to do.

I am here because I have to be.

I am doing this because I have no other choice.

I repeat those words out loud, for my own benefit, as I walk across the lounge, towards the door of Michelle Crane's office.

I can only assume that everything I need is in that room.

Taking a deep breath, I push down the handle, and step inside.

The centrepiece desk looks intimidating today, here alone. On my first visit, it seemed impressive, but now, it's overwhelming, stark, and cold, rather than stylish and uncomplicated. I look away, taking in the rest of the room, wondering where to start.

One wall is lined with filing cabinets, tall, dark wood, and obviously expensive looking. By the door there's a floor-to-ceiling storage cupboard, and the other walls, in the spaces between the tall windows, are lined with bookshelves. It's the kind of office anyone would dream of having.

The filing cabinets aren't labelled on the outside. I guess that Michelle and Hester know how their system works, so unattractive labelling would be superfluous for them. For me, though, it would be helpful to know where I should start to look for what it is that I need to find.

It's all here somewhere; I know only because I've been told that.

It's all here somewhere.

I have three days to find what I have been sent here for, but I'd be happier completing my mission right now.

I need to locate the information that will bring down Michelle Crane. Not because I want to, not because I have anything against her, but because I have to.

If I don't destroy Michelle Crane's life, I could lose everything.

Everything.

There are several documents that I've been tasked to find: tax papers, bank statements, identity records, anything that could be used to steal Michelle Crane's identity. Michelle must have her passport with her for her flight, so that's one option down.

I don't know anything about how they will be used when I find them. I'm a house sitter, not a criminal, although I suppose what I am doing contradicts that. This is something I would never do unless my life depended upon it, and unfortunately for Michelle Crane, it does.

The thing about identity is that it is so fragile. Michelle has built her public persona, that out-facing expression of her identity the world laps up. I'm here to pick at the meat of her *private* character. I need to dig up the bones of the real Michelle Crane and take them away with me. What happens then is out of my hands.

I've been told that what I need are physical documents. Michelle has built her empire on paper. Her room is lined with filing cabinets. I put two and two together and hope that she practices what she preaches. She must have hard copies. I just have to find them.

As the room itself was unlocked, so are the filing cupboards. I've come prepared, so before I touch anything, I pull a pair of thin cotton gloves from my pocket and put them on. Then I tug at the top drawer on the unit next to the window.

In the nerve-buzzing tension of the moment, I use too much force, and stumble back slightly. I almost fall onto the table. I right myself in time and make a mental note to be more cautious as I proceed. If I do my job properly, Michelle shouldn't even notice that I've been here. I've got no business being in her office, on the face of it. If I knock things over or cause any damage, it'll be a telltale sign that something's not right. I have to be more careful. There's no wiggle room for mistakes.

Idiot, I tell myself.

I step back up to the cabinet, pull again, with less vigour, and stare at the suspended files inside.

In a world that's becoming paper-free, Michelle is certainly on brand with her reams of documents. Storing hard copies might be going out of fashion, but that's one trend that Michelle isn't keeping up with. On one hand, it means that I might find what I am looking for. On the other, it means I can't type my search request into a digital input box and wait for a computer to show me where to head in the archives. If what I am looking for is here, I need to find it myself.

This could take a while.

I have three days.

I need to start looking now.

I flick through the files and pull one out at random. It's useless, and I push it back, careful to replace it exactly as I found it. If there's a system here, I'd better work it out.

I open another drawer, hoping to at least find something in the ballpark of what I need. As I slide the documents towards me and trace my finger along the tabs, something makes me stop dead in my tracks.

A noise from behind me. Not in this room, and not, I think, in the living room. The front door? Could it possibly be?

There's a clicking sound that I can definitely place as coming from the hallway, followed by a voice calling, "Hello?"

EIGHT

Libby

Three days into my new posting at Maynard Brookes, a sweet little accountancy firm twenty minutes away from home, and I've already run into a limpet. I'd love to be the person I used to be, and not give her a negative nickname just for being friendly, but I have to distance myself physically and emotionally, so I do what helps me to cope.

I get a blast of cheap body spray coming towards me before I see the girl entering the tiny printer room. She's one of those dress for the job you want types: a pencil skirt and matching suit jacket that she probably has dry-cleaned every week. The rest of the office team wears a smart casual mix of Shein-a-like work gear, and this one stands out in the crowd. Still, I can't remember her name. Abigail? Alison?

"I'm heading down to Coffee Express at lunchtime," she says.

"Right," I reply, turning to deal with an imaginary paper jam.

"I can wait for you if you'd like company."

She's persistent, I'll give her that.

"I brought lunch," I lie. "Thanks though."

I can feel her smiling at me, even though I've opened the front door of the printer and stuck my head as far away from her as I can.

"It's sticky sometimes," she says, leaning over me, brushing against my arm.

I flinch, drawing back from her in a jolt that has me crashing into the metal framed shelf beside me. A poorly stacked pile of papers tumbles down from above on top of me, fluttering to the ground by my feet.

"Oh, I'm sorry," she says, bending to pick up the mess that only I am responsible for.

"No, really, it was all me," I say, squatting to help her.

As she reaches one way and I lean the other, she collides with my arm again and this time I yelp before I can stop myself.

"Are you okay?" she asks, with a look of genuine concern. I haven't seen anyone look me like that for such a long time, and I'm almost shocked into giving an honest answer. I'm not okay. I'm not okay.

"Fine," I snap instead. I'm being too harsh, and I realise it as her expression changes. "I'm sorry," I say. "I have work to do. Do you mind...?" I gesture to the papers on the floor, and she shakes her head.

"No, of course," she says in her saccharine sweet voice.

There's something about her that makes me feel heart-breakingly sad. I think it's the fact that under other circumstances I really believe that she and I could have been friends.

I snatch my documents from the printer and force myself out of the room, leaving Amy, that's her name, on the floor, scrabbling to clear up my mess.

When I'm sure I'm out of her line of vision, I rub at my shirt sleeve, trying to soothe the ache in the bruises below the silk.

Imagine if I could accept Amy's offer, go out for lunch with a girl from work, maybe make a friend for once. Imagine if my life could be that easy.

One advantage of being a contractor is that I never spend too long in the same place. There's no need to form those awkward friendships with co-workers. The kind of casual rejection that I fobbed Amy off with has become second nature to me.

Apart from the standard end-of-project invitations, I usually get left out of social plans, anyway. Most of the people in the office would have to squint at my temporary ID badge to know my name. With that lack of intimacy comes personal security. Without reaching a certain level of perceived friendship, asking questions about my home life is off-limits.

What happens at home stays at home. All any of the office workers need to know is that I am a highly qualified, experienced, well presented professional, with a proven track record in getting results. That's what it says on my LinkedIn profile, and it's backed up by my actions.

Rather than coming across as stand-offish, I try to present an air of detachment. It's not that

I don't want to get to know people, rather it's that I don't want to form close bonds with colleagues that I am not likely to ever see again after my two or three months with them is up. Or at least that's what I want them to think. I smile at the appropriate times and answer any questions as vaguely as I can. I'm polite but put effort into maintaining a cool air of social indifference. Enigmatic, rather than rude: that's the image I try to portray.

If you think that I'm an antisocial bitch, you're wrong.

I used to have friends. I used to go to dinner parties, book clubs, but now…now I have nothing.

Trying to get other people to understand that is a different matter. I guess Amy won't bother asking me again now that I've turned her down. Best-case scenario, she'll go away to the other office workers and tell them what a cow I am. None of them will put any effort into trying to befriend me after Amy debriefs them in the coffee room. I can only hope that this is one of those gossipy places. Close colleagues, tight-knit workplace; no room for outsiders who think they're better than everyone else.

But of course, I don't.

I don't think that at all.

I know I am weak, pathetic, and useless.

No matter how many companies I have helped to turn themselves around. No matter what my references say about me ("Inspirational!", "Indispensable!"). I know what I am.

NINE

Jude

The voice in the hallway is instantly recognisable, even though I only heard it for the first time a few hours ago. It's Hester. She must have forgotten something. She's back already?

Stupidly, I had assumed that Michelle's angel would have been accompanying her on the trip. Surely if she was staying back, she could have watched the house. There was no need to hire me if Little Miss Do-Everything was around. My mind is switching to a panicked defensive state, but I need to stay focused and think now.

I stop dead and look around me.

I was methodological in my searching, and to the untrained eye nothing appears to have been disturbed. However, I don't have any good reason for being in here. I can't concoct an excuse that would make any kind of sense.

The only way out of here is through the door that leads back into the living area, and if Hester has already entered the house, unless she goes straight upstairs or through to the kitchen, that's exactly where she's going to be.

My eyes dart around the room. I could duck under the desk. If she walks in, she wouldn't see me unless she came around to Michelle's chair. There's no reason she would unless she was looking for me. The stationery cupboards aren't big enough for me to climb inside, so they aren't viable options. The curtains stop two feet short of the floor, so there's no way that I could stand behind them like a villain in a low-budget suspense movie.

I've got to think faster. I can hear footsteps in the hall now.

The curtains are a no-no, but the windows? Perhaps I could pop one open and duck out.

We're on the ground floor. The sash and slide design is perfect; I'm sure I can slip through.

"Jude?" I make an educated guess she's standing at the bottom of the stairs, as she calls my name.

I try to push the window up, feel the resistance and open the latch, and try again.

The window opens just far enough for me to duck the top half of my body through and clumsily force myself out into the garden.

I spin and press my hands against the frame, sliding the window back closed behind me.

Crap, crap, crap.

What now? Where to go? There's nowhere obvious that I can hide. I haven't had a chance to explore the grounds yet, so Hester has the home advantage. I've got to go with what I can see and blend in.

There's a wrought-iron bench at the edge of the lawn, and I take a quick look around, checking no one's watching, before I walk over briskly, and settle myself upon it.

Adrenaline is pumping through my system after my clumsy escape, and I try to calm my nerves. Slow, easy breaths. I need to look relaxed, as though I've been sitting here soaking in the view rather than ferreting through her boss's private belongings.

I hear the crunch of footsteps on the gravel behind me.

"Hey," a voice says. "Jude."

I turn my head and see Hester approaching. It's the first time I've had a chance to take in her appearance properly. She's such a plain, normal-looking woman. Not at all the type of person who I would expect Michelle Crane to associate with. I have to remind myself that Hester is staff, not one of Michelle's friend group. I've never seen Hester on any of Michelle's social media posts, and I think I understand why.

"Oh," I say, trying to sound surprised to see her. "Hi."

I stop there, deciding to let her do the talking.

"Everything okay?" she asks, walking around to stand by the side of the bench.

"Sure," I smile.

They left how long ago? Five hours? A little less? It's an hour and a half to the airport. Hester must have seen Michelle through security before she came back here unless she dropped her and went somewhere else. The second explanation seems unlikely though. I get the feeling that Hester spends most of her waking hours in Michelle's company.

She pauses, looking me up and down.

"Are you sure?" She eyes me. "You seem a little flustered for someone who's sitting in such a peaceful garden."

I try not to frown; I thought my play acting was on point.

"It's an exquisite garden," I admit. "And I was...I'm just surprised to see you," I say, without needing to lie. "I thought you were going with Michelle."

Hester laughs. "I see." She reaches into her pocket, pulls out a packet of cigarettes and offers the pack to me.

I wave my hand in a *no*.

Hester lights up and blows a plume of smoke away from me.

"I can't stand flying," she says. "All that time cooped up in a little box in the air, and nowhere to do the things I love." She takes another long drag as though illustrating her point. "No, thank you."

"Doesn't Michelle need you?"

"I get some time off," Hester says, the trace of laughter not quite leaving her voice. "We aren't joined at the hip, you know; despite what assumptions you may have made."

"I haven't. I mean, I didn't. I…" I shake my head. "I don't know what you mean." I do though. I can work it out just fine.

Hester puts the cigarette to her lips and nods. That's enough.

"Can I ask why, er, why she needs a house sitter if you aren't going away with her?"

"I have other stuff to do," Hester says. "I don't want to be stuck here all week, no matter how *dazzling* Michelle's pad is. I spend enough time here when she's around. I don't need to be here when she isn't."

And yet here you are, I think but don't say.

"I thought I'd check how you were settling in, and I need to pick up a few things." Hester gives me that look again and continues. "I'll pop back a few times while you're here." She pauses for another drag on her cigarette before speaking again. "In case you need anything." The emphasis on the last words leaves me with no doubt that Hester intends to check up on me.

Have it your way, I think. She's made a mistake by letting me know that she'll be coming over. Forewarned is forearmed and all that. Now I know that there's a chance I could be interrupted, I'll just have to be more careful.

"Well, I'm sure I'll be fine," I say as sweetly as possible, trying to maintain this pretence we are building, "but thanks."

I'm not used to having anyone else around while I'm sitting. One part of the job I particularly enjoy is being left to my own devices. Moving from house to house is unsettling, no matter how much I like what I do. I need space to settle and relax in a new environment. Especially now, with the task that I need to complete.

I can't help but wonder why Hester wants to monitor me. Michelle obviously trusts me, she picked me from the available applicants and welcomed me with open arms, but Hester? I'm getting an unsettling vibe from her.

It would be helpful to know exactly when I can expect to see Hester again, but there's no way to ask without making myself sound suspicious. This is a minor hiccup, that's all. I can deal with it. I have to.

"Come with me," Hester says suddenly, reaching out a hand to help me to my feet.

"Uh, okay," I reply.

I don't have any option other than to follow her as she leads me around the side of the building, back to the front door. She crunches the last quarter of her cigarette beneath her expensive-looking shoe, into the gravel. Then she pushes the door, taking me through into the hallway, and on to the living room.

Passing a brief glance in my direction, she lets go of my hand at last and pushes open the door to Michelle's study.

My heart thunders. Did she know I was in there after all?

"Come in," she says, walking into Michelle's room.

"Are you sure?"

"She's not here," Hester says with a shrug. "I don't think you have anything to worry about."

Worry about? I'm trying my best to look indifferent, let alone worried.

As though reading my mind, Hester laughs.

"Relax. It's not some kind of sacred ground. I just want to borrow a pen."

"Right," I smile.

Hester reaches into the cupboard closest to the door and fishes around in a mug that's filled with pens and pencils. Then she scrawls on a Paper Crane brand post-it, and peels off the note to pass to me.

"My number," she says. "Any problem, call me. Okay?"

"Okay," I reply, trying to hide my bemusement.

I can't imagine that I would ever want to phone Hester, but she's making it look like she's doing me a big favour, so I accept the paper and smile.

"I'm going to head off now," she says, resting her hand against the doorframe.

"Well, thanks."

She came back just to give me her number? It would have been much easier for her to let me have it when she was here earlier. Surely there's no reason that she would want to keep this a secret from Michelle. That's the only thing I can think of, and it makes no sense.

It's not quite the only thing.

The other explanation is, of course, that she came back to check up on me. She wanted to pop her head in to see what I was up to and make sure I wasn't doing anything nefarious. But Michelle has entrusted this house to my care. Michelle trusts me, that's the bottom line. It doesn't really matter what Hester thinks. I don't have to prove myself to her.

On the other hand, she could make things difficult for me if she suspects anything. I need to keep her on side, regardless.

"That's so nice of you," I smile. "Thanks, Hester."

She smiles back, and although we are standing in Michelle's office, two women working for the same employer for a short time, one of us wants to protect Michelle Crane, and the other is planning to ruin her life. If Hester knew what I was about to do, she would never leave me alone in this room.

But leave me alone is what she does.

She nods once, and then turns, walking out of the office, through to the hallway, and out of the front doors of the house.

I'm back where I started before she arrived, and a part of me has a niggling feeling that Hester knows that.

TEN

Even though I'm back in Michelle's office, something stops me from continuing the search straight away. I have a bad feeling that I can't put my finger on, but equally that I can't shake. Why did Hester bring me back to this room and leave me in here? She either knew that I was here when she arrived, or she's trying to give me a message of some kind. That it's okay to be in this room, or…what? She's trying to set me up? She wants to be able to tell Michelle that I was in here?

It's a lot easier to have paranoid thoughts when you've got something to hide. My mind can't dial it down to a more positive level at the moment, so instead, I give myself a brief break. I have a job to do, and I have to start soon, but first I need a few minutes to compose myself.

I decide to make coffee and fix myself one of those corned beef and tomato sandwiches that Michelle was raving about. I haven't eaten yet today, and the woozy light-headedness of my empty stomach can't be helping with my state of mind.

The kitchen is spotless, and I'm sure that I could eat directly off the granite worktop rather than opening cupboard after cupboard to find the crockery. Still, it takes me three doors before I pull out a square side-plate, and somehow my sandwich looks even more appetising once I've placed it upon the designer crockery. I almost want to pull out my phone and take a photograph.

And then I pause.

I pat my pant pockets.

My phone.

I don't have it.

When did I last…?

My mind races, trying to scroll back over my movements from the past hour. Office. Garden.

Did I have it when I went outside? Did I leave it in the office? Is that how Hester knew I was there? Has she taken it?

No, no, no.

I feel a heavy thud in my gut, and instead of hunger, I'm gripped by nausea and push the plate along the counter away from me.

How could I have been so stupid? I left my phone on the office desk. I must have done. It's not as though there's anything else there to hide it. Of course, Hester would see it if I left it on the desk. Giving me her number was a cute little dig at me. How can I possibly call her if she has my phone.

She has my phone.

The thought sends me into a deep panic. I need that phone. I need to remain available.

If I don't answer...

If I don't tell them what they need to hear...

Crap, crap, crap.

I've completely screwed myself.

My skin is practically prickling with tension.

An ominous thumping resonates in my chest, a haunting rhythm of fear.

No, no, no.

This can't be happening. This is my first day here. My first chance to...

And then it hits me.

I had the phone upstairs, in the bedroom, before I even started to search the office. They phoned me, and I answered, and I…

It must still be up there.

I race out of the kitchen, back into the hallway, and take the stairs two at a time, not thinking about the risk of slipping and falling. Not now. There's no time for such trivial concerns when my entire life is riding on finding that phone.

As I hit the top stair, I misjudge my step and stumble forwards, throwing my hands out in front of me onto the landing to break my fall, hoping beyond hope I land on the carpet instead of banging back onto the staircase behind me. My right elbow twists sharply beneath my weight, and I let out an expletive, safe in the knowledge that no one can hear me.

Despite the jagged pain darting up my arm, I land safely on the upstairs carpet, only the lower part of my legs dangling over the marble stairs. The knee that I banged in the bathroom earlier tries to complain after this second insult, but the aching in my elbow is stronger.

Could have been worse, I tell myself with more than a hint of snark, as I pull my body up to a standing position.

What if I had fallen downstairs? No one would find me until, well, whenever Hester decided to show up again. I don't want her here, but it strikes me she might be an important lifeline. In two years of house-sitting, I have never run into any kind of trouble, but this time is different. I'm not here to relax and enjoy the experience of being in a stranger's home. I'm here to save my own ass.

So.

My phone.

I give my elbow a brisk rub, which doesn't help at all, but at least it's something, and I walk quickly towards my bedroom. No more running, no more falling, no more being an idiot. I have to focus.

Lack of focus made me misplace my phone.

Lack of focus made me slip on the stairs.

Lack of focus could cost me everything.

When I push open the door to the guest room and see my travel bag sitting on the bed, I get a strange feeling of reassurance. Here, in this strange place, there's something that belongs to me. Somehow, this room feels like my private sanctum within Michelle's mansion. I've stayed in houses where the owners haven't had spare rooms and have instead changed their sheets and let me sleep in their own beds. I've stayed in houses where I had to take a duvet out to the sofa and make do with the discomfort of curling up in the living room for a week. My room here feels special; I wish I deserved it.

I don't have time to think any more about that now. I need to find my phone.

Even though I don't expect to find it there, I rifle around in my bag, taking out the few items of clothing that I brought with me and laying them onto the bed. May as well unpack while I'm looking. Pants, pyjamas, socks. Blah, blah, blah. Maybe I'll hang my T-shirt up in the armoire later, just for the hell of it.

I squat down on the floor next to the bed, feeling my hands sink into the deep pile of the carpet, and look underneath. There's nothing down there at all; no boxes stored away like there are in my flat. I have to use every inch of space available. Michelle has the luxury of square footage. If I had as much room as she did, I'm sure I could be a lot tidier than I am. The tidiness means that I can see that my phone is definitely not hiding under the bed.

There's only one place I haven't looked: the en suite.

As soon as I push the door open, I see it, face down on the tiled floor.

Don't be cracked, I silently pray. *Don't be broken.*

But it's not.

And it's here.

No need to panic. No harm done. And as I look at the screen, I see there are no missed calls.

I let out a sighed breath of relief.

Flipping down the toilet lid, I take a seat. Of all the places in this house that I could sit, this is no doubt the least luxurious, but I need a moment to recover.

It's been two weeks since I received the first phone call from the unknown number, and I've been on edge ever since. I can never be too far from my mobile because I never know when it's going to ring. If I don't answer, if I don't tell them what they want to hear, my life as I know it could be over. I'm completely under the control of someone that I have never met, and probably never will.

It seems unimaginable to think that something like this could happen to someone like me, but then again, I couldn't have imagined a lot of the things that have happened to me over the past few years. No matter how bad my life has been, though, I know that if I don't carry out my mission here, my life is going to get much, much worse.

ELEVEN

Libby

The incident in the print room has knocked me off track. I know this because half an hour later in the break room, I find myself pouring cold water over my tea bag from a kettle I've forgotten to switch on. The worst of it is that I don't notice until I've added milk, sat back at my hot-seat desk, and taken a hefty swig. It's disgusting and I gasp, spraying cold beige liquid over the papers that I've only just printed.

Instinctively, I look around to check that nobody has seen me. I'm a specialist consultant and my reputation depends upon me presenting a professional image. I need to influence the company that I am being employed by to believe in me and my work. They're not likely to do that if they see the spluttering mess that I've let myself become just because someone tried to be friendly towards me.

I pull open my Tumi Voyageur – a bag that I would like to say that I chose for function over prestige – and rifle through the contents for a pack of tissues.

I've just managed to pull one out and start dabbing at the documents when I hear a burst of laughter from across the top of my cubicle. I hate these things, these compartmentalising boxes that office workers have to sit in. Luckily, a lot of companies are switching to desk spaces without these barriers between colleagues, but some places, like this one, think that privacy – or segregation – has some kind of benefit for productivity. Much as I don't want to (can't) socialise with my so-called co-workers, I hate being shut off like this. It's cold and claustrophobic.

It also means that I can't see who is laughing, or what they find so funny. The sound jolts me, and my insecure brain immediately thinks that the girl is laughing at me. Has someone seen what I've done? I snap my head around, checking that there's no one behind me, watching, gloating over my mistake. As I turn, I kick the wastebasket beneath my desk, tipping it and spilling the contents over the floor. Balled paper, an empty cup from Coffee Express, and a couple of post-it notes tumble out and I can feel my face glowing with embarrassment at my stupidity. Perhaps those barriers are a good thing after all.

There's another peel of laughter, shrill and too loud, from across the room. Before I bend to scoop up the contents of the bin, I pop my head over the parapet.

Amy and two of the other girls are in a huddle. As I look up, across towards them, the taller of the three nudges Amy, and nods in my direction. There's no attempt at discretion, no hint of trying to disguise the movement, and when Amy turns to look at me, it's patently clear that I most definitely am the source of their amusement.

I want to maintain eye contact with Amy, stand my ground with some kind of defiant gesture, but instead I dip my head, hiding from their stares.

I'm a professional woman, a specialist in my field. I've been headhunted by this company to develop infrastructure changes that are likely to improve the functioning of this organisation, and, as a knock-on effect of that, the working lives of those three witches over there. I should have their respect. Hell, I should have their appreciation for what I am doing here. But I don't fit in. I can't fit in. Whatever *they* expect of me, I just can't deliver.

I'll carry on with my work, and in four weeks' time I'll make the end of project presentation and change everything for the better apart from my own life.

Across the room, the laughter has settled to a low hum of chatter. I can't pick out any of the words, but I'm sure they are still discussing what a snobbish, uppity cow I am. I don't have the luxury of being able to sit here and feel sorry for myself. I have to focus on the job before me.

The spreadsheet on the screen in front of me swims with highlighted text fields and figures. All those pound signs; money that I could never imagine. If I had that kind of money, I could change my own life. I could finally be free. Free from the need to turn down every offer of social interaction. Free from his control. Free.

And that's when the plan starts to shape itself in my mind. The numbers on the screen dance around before me in a Fantasia-like performance. Money. That's what I need. If I had…how much? I wouldn't need anything extravagant, just enough to set me up and get me started. Rent for a month or two, and the deposit to go with it. Food, bills, no luxuries. I could get by on the minimum until I got the next wages through. A smile breaks across my face as I imagine what it might be like to have my own money paid into my own bank account; what it might be like to be financially independent; what it might be like to be free.

If Amy and her friends are still talking, I don't hear them. I'm opening another spreadsheet, making different kinds of calculations.

If I can save companies, surely I can save myself.

I just need to work out how.

TWELVE

Jude

I'm tempted to run a bath, use some of the Diptyque bath gel Michelle has thoughtfully provided and let myself sink beneath the bubbles for a while. If this were any other assignment, if I wasn't here to find personal documents to pass on to my anonymous caller, I would be doing just that. I don't have a bath in my pokey flat, so even without the exquisite scents, bathing is a luxury. I make an unspoken deal with myself that if I get on with the job, dig out those papers and make my first outgoing call to the cursed number, if I do that, I'll let myself relax. Once the dirty work is out of the way, I'll have the rest of the time to enjoy being here. Somehow, I doubt that I'll be much in the mood for relaxation with the burden of knowing what I have done.

Either way, I can't stay in the bathroom forever, so I stand up and push the phone into my pocket.

I need to be more careful.

I watch my step on the stairs as I make my way back down. It's late evening now, and although it's not yet dark in the hallway, the change in the way the light falls at this time of the day is noticeable. The open plan living area benefits from the daylight coming from the impressive glazing, but the only natural light in the atrium comes from two arched windows, one to either side of the entrance.

There are three long mirrors hanging on the wall to my right as I walk towards the great room, but I don't want to look at myself. Even though I know that I have to do what it is expected of me here, my gut still churns with the thought of the consequences.

As I've learned to my detriment, every action can lead to consequences. A simple solution to a major problem might not always be as simple as it first seems. It's not that I believe in Karma or anything like that, because I really wouldn't be here planning to take down Michelle Crane if I did. What kind of spiritual comeuppance would I get for doing such a crappy thing? I can't begin to imagine.

I'm in this situation, being subjected to this whole shitshow, because of a decision I made. You never know exactly what you'll do until the chips are down, your back's up against the wall, and all those other cliches that you would never believe could ring true - until they actually do.

What I have to do right now is to find those documents.

I would love to stop in the living room, curl up on that soft velvet sofa where I sat opposite Michelle only a few days ago. I didn't have time to appreciate it properly, with the nervous energy of the almost-interview and the knowledge of what it would mean if I didn't get the job. I was prepared to beg and plead, in the most professional way possible, in order to win Michelle over. How lucky I was that she had already made her decision.

Something about how easy it was pulls me up in my tracks. Me being here is all part of my caller's plan. They must have known that my references would get me this job. I wonder for a moment how many other Homesitters employees they background checked before they singled me out. Michelle's data is their end goal, but first they had to find their weapon, and there had to be some ammunition. Surely nobody would do what I am about to do without having a compelling reason to do so. What kind of person could destroy a stranger, unprovoked. Michelle seems, from the little that I have seen of her, like a benevolent individual.

Again, I get that wrenching feeling of guilt choking in my throat. I don't want this. I don't want to do this. But there's so much at stake that I have no other option.

I walk past the comfort of the sofa, towards the door to Michelle's office, and push it open.

Back in front of the filing cabinets, gloves on, I decide to start at the other end of the row. There didn't seem to be anything relevant in the file I flicked through before Hester arrived, so it makes sense to look elsewhere.

As I open the drawer and finger through the paperwork, I run over in my mind what it is that I'm looking for. Tax documents, bank statements, anything with personal identification details. I wouldn't have a clue what to do with any of those papers myself. How do you even go about stealing someone's identity or defrauding them or whatever it is my caller plans to do? I'm the weapon. I don't need to know what damage is going to be caused. I'm trying my best not to think about it.

My job is to find what my caller wants.

My job is to save myself.

I've already scanned through the upper drawer while my thoughts have been ticking over. Nothing but invoices. I wonder whether they would be of any use if I can't find the exact documents that I've been tasked with recovering. Can you extract any data from invoices? I pull one out and read it. Michelle's business address – here. We already knew that. A reference number. Details of a sale made, the amount paid, and the purchaser. So what? I shove the paper back into the drawer, and then correct myself, straightening it so that no one would ever notice that it had been removed.

Sometime soon, Michelle is going to realise what has happened. I'm sure she is going to realise who did this to her, but as I have no motive, and none of the financial benefits will be traceable to me, I can't let myself worry about repercussions. You can't blame a gun for the murder.

THIRTEEN

Document after document, all I am seeing are sales invoices. Why Michelle keeps hard copies of all these papers is beyond me. Many of them have evidently been received electronically, and Michelle has printed them out to store them here. Paper Crane is a hugely successful business, and for a brand this popular, I know there must be countless office workers and underlings based elsewhere. There's no way that Michelle's empire is a one-woman enterprise.

That's the image that she wants to portray on social media though. Paper Crane is all about the woman behind the business. It's her concept, her designs, her dedication and hard work that have got her to where she is today. Michelle *is* Paper Crane. The social media posts, with not-so-subtle product placement in exotic locations and airport lounges around the world, parties, sleek, stylish images that show you, the normal woman, that you too could live this kind of life if you would only choose Paper Crane products – all of that branding is centred upon Michelle and her oh-so-perfect life.

Rather than hate her for the image of perfection that she pedals, though, people love her. It's inspirational, rather than irritating. When I think of Michelle Crane, I'm not envious of her lifestyle, I'm impressed by what she has achieved. Or at least that's how I felt up until a few weeks ago. Once I knew what I had to do, all that changed. How could I screw her over while still seeing her as an empowering entrepreneur?

Don't think about that, I tell myself, and slam the bottom drawer closed.

I'm getting nowhere.

I let myself sink to the floor beside the cabinet and flop my hands onto my knees as I survey the room.

Directly in front of me is the desk. My caller told me not to touch the computer, and with so much at stake, I'm glad of having one less place to search. What if I just can't find what I'm looking for here? Surely the deal with my caller must be off. They can't expect me to produce something that doesn't exist. I can't be held accountable for that. They can't…

As my mind races, my heartbeat follows suit. I know that if I overthink this, panic is going to sweep in, and I won't be able to focus on what I have to do. I've got to keep a clear head, and I need to do what I was sent here for. I can't assume that somebody who is willing to bring down an innocent woman would be particularly understanding if I failed them.

The only other place I can search in this room are the cupboards.

But what if the documents aren't here at all?

If – as is most likely – Michelle has business premises elsewhere, couldn't her personal paperwork be kept there? Why would she leave identification and financial credentials around her home, especially when she doesn't seem bothered about having a better security system than some random woman that works for an online house-sitting site?

I can't stop the thought that enters my head.

Dumb ass, I think. *If you can't protect yourself more carefully, you deserve what you get.*

Even though I didn't speak the words out loud, I clap my hand over my mouth, ashamed by the thought.

I'm in this situation because I didn't protect myself more carefully. There's no way that I can judge Michelle Crane, and I can't pass off my guilt at what I am doing here by victim shaming.

Michelle doesn't deserve to have her life ruined.

But neither do I.

I allow myself a few more moments of reflection and rest before pulling myself up to my feet and continuing the search. I don't know why I thought it was going to be easy, walking in here, picking out the papers I needed and letting my caller know the job was done. I suppose the alternative was too bleak to think about, but the more time I spend searching, the greater the danger is that I'm going to fail.

The caller.

My blackmailer.

A nameless adversary.

It all sounds so terribly clichéd, but if I knew who it was that was doing this, perhaps I could have found another way out.

This whole nightmare began less than a month ago. I was house-sitting for a lovely elderly couple, a week by the sea in a picture-postcard cottage in the west of Dorset. Two cats (*Diana* and *Camilla*) to feed, neither of whom hung around to socialise with me once their bowls had been filled. That was the kind of peaceful life I opted for when I started this line of work. The last thing I expected was that it could be an avenue to becoming a pawn in a malevolent person's nefarious schemes.

I'd been out for a walk, trying to make the most of the sunshine by the cliffs, when globules of rain began to splatter around me. Just a few at first; huge, but well-spaced warnings of what was to come. I hadn't taken a coat, but when the sky darkened and the clouds opened, I pulled my cardigan uselessly over my head and ran back to the cottage.

The cats were already sitting on the mat outside the cottage, giving me the side-eye as I dashed up the path and rattled the unfamiliar key in the lock. The two of them mewled as my clumsiness kept us out in the downpour for longer than necessary, and raced into the warm, safe house ahead of me as I finally managed to fling the door open.

"You're welcome," I muttered as the wet cats leapt onto the sofa.

I settled onto the less-comfortable chaise, accepting my place, and pulled a crocheted blanket over me.

I was just warming up when my phone rang.

For someone who has few friends and no family to speak of, hearing the ringtone coming from my pocket usually means only one of two things. Or at least it did then. Work or spam. Like most people, I let unknown callers tumble straight to voicemail, but with my line of employment, I answer pretty much everything else.

It was a mobile number, no identifiable location, but that was usual for the kind of calls I received. I picked up, and I've regretted that moment ever since.

I don't have time to think about that now. There are two cupboards, each double-doored, on the wall opposite the filing cabinets. One wall is lined with cupboards, one is a pattern of bookshelf-window-bookshelf-window, one is lined with files. The last wall, of course, houses the windows that I was climbing out of earlier this afternoon. Despite the passing hours, this room is still well-lit by the evening sunshine filtering into the room. I can see why Michelle chose this location as her office.

When I open the first cupboard, I know immediately that I won't find what I'm looking for in there. It's filled with stationery supplies and samples – all emblazoned with that quirky Paper Crane origami logo. I wonder for a split second whether Michelle would notice if I helped myself to a notepad or one of the new, unused notebooks. Of course, I can't do that. I'm wearing gloves so that I don't leave fingerprints – leaving evidence that I've stolen stationery is the last thing I want to do. Still, the beautiful pastel designs are a sweet temptation. I can see why people buy so many of these things. Right now, though, they aren't helping me.

I step back, irritated, and try to slam the door. However, I'm thwarted by the sleek design of the furniture, as it slides to a slow closure despite my efforts. That's probably for the best. I should be more careful. I should stay in control of my feelings.

Before I even look inside the final cupboard, I have a heart-sinking feeling that I'm not going to find what I need in there.

I'm right.

The shelves are filled with more blank sheets of paper, note blocks, a long line of tapes on stylish dispensers, boxes of Paper Crane branded pens. Nothing of any use to me at all.

Shit.

Even though it looks obvious that what I want isn't hidden inside the cupboard, I search thoroughly, just to be sure. This is too important to be glib about.

Still, I find nothing.

If the papers that I need are in this house, they aren't in this room.

The bookshelves only contain books. Unless Crane has gone to the effort of hiding each of her personal documents inside one of those volumes, I'm not going to find them there. I pause in front of the shelves, contemplating whether that's a possibility. Is it possible? Yes. Is it probable? I'm going with no. If I can't find what I need elsewhere, I'll come back and pull down every single book.

Shit, shit, shit.

There's only one place – other than the computer – that I haven't looked, and I only know that it exists because Michelle showed me: the drawer on the desk. Without knowing it was there, the sleek design makes it look as though the compartment is part of the desk itself. I would never have thought to look there if it wasn't for her.

Perhaps that's a sign, I think, optimistically or desperately, I'm no longer sure which.

I tug on the sleeves of my gloves, making sure they are secure, but also because of my nervous tension. My fingers are tingling, I need to stay steady.

I'm about to press the hidden button and pull open the drawer when I hear a noise.

Or I think I do.

I can't be sure. I don't know if it's because I'm so on edge and I'm imagining things, or if there's someone there. Would Hester come back again so soon? Is anyone else likely to visit? Michelle didn't mention anyone, but then again, she didn't tell me that Hester would be hanging around either.

I almost call out a shuddering *hello*.

But I'm in Michelle's office, and I don't have any particularly good reason for being here. My mind is so frazzled that I doubt my skills to think something up on the spot, so instead, I remain silent and listen. If someone tries to come into the house, I will hear them.

A minute passes. I wait longer. I wait until I am sure that I'm alone, and then, slowly, I press the button that releases the drawer.

Junk.

All I find inside the drawer is junk.

A couple of pens, a stapler, a small bottle of Penhaligon's Orange Blossom perfume, and at the back a raggedy origami crane. A real-world embodiment of the Paper Crane logo. Cute, but useless.

It's either time to start pulling down the paperbacks or to make a plan for exploring the rest of the house, because one thing is for certain – Michelle's secrets are not hidden here.

FOURTEEN

My grumbling stomach reminds me I never finished making that sandwich, after I was rudely interrupted by my paranoid mind. It's almost nine o'clock, according to the digital display in the office. I haven't eaten since breakfast, mainly because of the stress of knowing what I have to do here. I decide to make my way through to the kitchen, eat, and have a quick search in there, just in case. I can't imagine that anyone would store important documents in their food cupboards or fridge, but wouldn't that make it the perfect hiding place?

Michelle was right about the corned beef and tomato sandwiches. I make and eat one, and then a second; they're delicious. And my first assumption was correct about the kitchen. I open and close every cabinet and container: there's nothing there.

Still, that's one more room checked off the list. One step closer to failure, if I choose to look at it like that, but I can't afford to fail. I have to keep moving, keep searching. If I've got to tear this place apart, so be it. As long as I can piece it back together seamlessly once I've found what I'm looking for.

I pause and think. I don't have a notebook – Paper Crane or otherwise – and pen in front of me, so I try to visualise my plan forming in my head.

I have tonight, tomorrow, and some of the next day. Michelle is due home around three on Monday, so I can't afford to wait and leave it until the last minute. I need those last hours to make sure that everything looks spotless and untouched. Best bet: keep searching tonight until I find the papers. If I have to stay up all night, so be it. I started looking in what I thought was the most obvious place, and I seem to have moved on to the least obvious, if you discount the bathrooms. I mentally catalogue the other rooms. Downstairs: the open plan living room, atrium and the two rooms that Michelle dismissed on our walking tour as *'storage, more storage'*. Upstairs, I have barely investigated. Crane said that there are five bedrooms, and I assume they all have their own bathrooms. I'm already fairly certain that every storage space in my room is empty – even under the bed. A flicker of hope ignites in me that the other guest suites will also be shells, ready-prepared for the countless guests that Michelle must invite over on the weekends that she's in town.

If I were a millionaire businesswoman jetsetter, where would I store my personal paperwork?

I wash my plate and knife and stand them on the drying rack beside the sink as I toss the thought over in my mind.

I already know that my answer would not be *inside my home in a place where random strangers could find it and use it against me.*

My caller said that the documents are here. They are certain enough of that fact to have sent me, and to be holding me personally responsible for finding them, so I have to believe it.

Whoever is out to get Michelle knows a lot about her. I don't know what their motive is, and I haven't stopped to think about it. The less I know about the plan behind the entire scheme the better.

"I have a job for you."

That's how it began.

When I answered the phone call from the unrecognised number, that was the greeting.

"I have a job for you."

Not that unusual. I've been working as a house sitter for long enough that word gets around, even outside of my agency-scheduled jobs. A friend tells a friend. Word spreads when people find a reliable house sitter. That's why references are so vital in this line of work. It's all about getting people to trust you. I've never done anything, not until now anyway, that would make me appear anything other than honest. Now I'm risking all of that, the reputation that I've built up, the years of work that I've put in. Not because I want to, but because I have to.

The voice sounded strange, but then, that first time, I didn't read too much into it. I didn't stop to think.

"Where are you located?" I asked, my tone casual but professional. I was still distracted by my escape from the rainstorm, and all I really wanted to do was relax and hope that one of the cats would come over and let me pet them.

"Well, Jude, dear. It's not that kind of job."

I pulled myself upright, almost involuntarily. I needed to focus, to pay attention, because as soon as my caller said that, something deep inside me detected things were about to take a dark turn. Just as a few drops of rain can be a warning of the coming storm, that short sentence was enough to warn me that shit was about to happen.

"Jude," the voice continued. "I believe you are in the perfect position to help me with a little problem that I have."

I waited, not knowing what to say, but also not wanting to interrupt.

"I need you to house-sit for me."

A wave of relief washed through my body. I'd got it all wrong, misread the situation. The pressure of the storm had got to me, and I was blowing things out of proportion. I was on edge, that was all.

I wish that had been correct.

"Not my house, though," the voice said. "I happen to know that a certain person is leaving the country for a few days. That certain person has something that I need."

That dark turn was becoming a reality. I wanted it to stop right there. I didn't want to hear any more.

"I'm sorry," I said, as politely as I could manage, under the circumstances. Just in case I had somehow misread the situation. "I won't be able to do that. Perhaps you could refer them to the Homesitter agency."

The caller actually laughed. It was a raspy, dry laugh that sounded as though it caused them pain to let it out. I was not seeing the funny side of it.

"It's not that kind of job," they said again. "Jude, I need you to listen." The words were hard now, harsher than before, and the light-hearted laugh had gone. "You are going to do this for me, because I know some things about you that could make your life very difficult if you don't."

My throat closed up. My eyes widened in sheer surprise at what I was hearing.

I knew it was possible, that one day someone might discover the truths that I had tried to bury, but I never imagined that someone could use them against me quite like this.

I couldn't speak, but there were no words that I could say anyway.

"That's right," my caller said. "I know everything. You see, I deal in information and identities. That's what I do. And Jude, my dear, you *are* going to help me."

Outside, a crash of thunder sounded, causing Camilla to mewl out a forlorn cry.

The caller's voice continued.

"Or I'm going to destroy you."

FIFTEEN

Libby

I'm sure that Amy and her friends would never imagine that someone like me, seemingly so confident, aloof, and stuck-up, could be in the situation that I am actually in. No one expects the high-flying alpha female to be subordinate in her own household. If I could actually talk to Amy – to any of them – and tell them about my home life, they wouldn't be clustering together, sharing their jokes at my expense.

I'm sure they would feel sorry for me, try to give me well-meaning advice that I'd never be able to take, or tell me I'm worth more than this and I should leave him.

Because it's that easy, isn't it?

Because of course I would have been letting this happen for the past five years because I want to.

Sure.

If it were so easy to leave, I would have walked away the first time that my husband, Neil, raised his hand to me. It wasn't a punch, then. It wasn't even a slap. It started with his hand around my wrist, just a little too tightly. We were in the supermarket; I never saw it as strange that he wanted to be with me every time I went out of the house. Silly old me thought it was romantic that he didn't want me out of his sight, couldn't bear to be without me. That's how dumb I was. I saw all the red flags and thought they were decorations, not warning signs.

Anyway, I walked down the magazine aisle.

"We don't need anything from down there," he said. I didn't even pick up on the tone in his voice. I didn't realise it was a command, rather than a passing statement.

"I'm just going to have a look at…"

Before I had a chance to finish my sentence, his hand was on my wrist, a soft pressure at first, but as I stepped away, it didn't let up. He tightened his grip.

"We don't need anything," he said again, his eyes boring into me in a way I hadn't seen before.

Or had I?

Had it been brewing ever since he lost his job and became the stay-at-home half of our relationship?

He was another casualty of a year from hell where companies failed, and we floundered to make our way through financial setbacks and the kind of life changes we could never have imagined. I worked from home, kept bringing in the pay cheques and my salary kept landing in our joint account. The world went back to near-normal; I could travel to the companies that I was working for again, but he had nothing to go back to. Neil was cooped up, still locked down, and I think that was when something inside him snapped.

At least that's when I started to see the changes.

He gripped my arm, and when I tried to laugh it off and pull away from him, still thinking that it was all some kind of strange game, he dug his fingertips into my flesh. A surge of fear and pain coursed through my body as his fingers clamped down on my wrist, his once familiar touch becoming a painful vice that constricted my flesh. I knew there would be bruising, and I'm embarrassed to say that my first thought was that someone was going to see it. I should have thought more about what that first low-level assault might lead to, but there I was, thinking about what people would think if they saw me with bruises on my wrist.

Remembering that now turns my stomach, but I soon found out that Neil was just as worried about what people would think. The punches, kicks and bites that followed, everything he did to me from that day until the most recent incident earlier this week, were all focused on areas that I could cover up with long sleeves, high necklines and as many lies and excuses as I could think of.

Perhaps if it was only physical, I could bear it. He doesn't go too far, only enough for me to get the message that he's in control. A part of me shouts up to be heard when I let myself think like that. Any abuse is too much, but it could be worse. I know other people face much worse. The argumentative side of me tries to remind me it's not a competition, that my experience is not any less important than anyone else's. I know. I know. But it's more than that. It's the control that he has over me that hurts the most. I have no financial freedom, everything I have goes to our joint account, which he sees as his personal income. I have no social life. I'm being treated like a pariah in the office directly because of how he controls me. Work is all I have. It's my only escape from him, and I can't feel like crap here too.

I need to think, and the way I think is through brainstorming. I've got the figures on the screen in front of me now. I know how much I need so that I can escape, but I don't know how to get it. I have to plan, and as a shit hot project manager, it should be no problem at all. Saving companies and saving myself are two different skills sets though.

Plan. I've got to plan. I take in a deep breath, stretch my arms out before me, and try to shake off the tension that's running through my body. This is what I do. I plan. I can do this.

Starting the way I always do when I begin a new project, I reach down into my bag for a second time and pull out my notepad. I can buy myself expensive stationery, clothes, and accessories, but I can't buy myself out of this life.

The time has come. I've had enough. It's hard enough having to endure the abuse at home; my workplaces were the only safe spaces I had. I constantly have to hide who I am, deny my own needs, avoid social interaction, and abide by the rules that *he* lays down for me. Until now, I thought there was no way out, but maybe, just maybe, there is.

I pick a pen up from my desk and begin to write.

Problem number one: I need money to be able to get away from my husband.
Problem number two: My salary is paid directly into our joint account.

When the words are written on the paper, I stare at them, as if by documenting the facts of my situation I'll be able to manifest a solution.

It doesn't work.

I switch out the black ink fountain pen for a fluorescent highlighter. That little origami crane icon is in flight on the logo that embellishes the lid, and somehow it feels like a sign. I could fly free, if only I could work out how to unfold my wings. If I could make paper work for me...

And then it hits me. There is a solution. There's one potentially simple way that I could solve my problems. I swipe the highlighter over the page, picking out the key words as I let my thoughts begin to crystallise and form the plan.

money
get away
account

If there was a way that I could obtain money that didn't go directly into our shared account, I could save enough to leave him. He wouldn't know until it was too late – until after I had gone far, far away. No forwarding address, no chance of knowing where I was, no way he could find me again. If I could just squirrel away enough, I could be free.

SIXTEEN

Jude

Searching the living area was easy. Michelle has opted for such a sleek, minimalistic approach to design that there are no stacks of paper hidden away in cupboards, no piles of magazines waiting for a trip to the recycling bin. Everything has its place, and the room is spotless to a T. The more time I spend in this house, the more envious I become. Living here would be so easy, so much more comfortable than my shabby flat, so much more space and light...

That thought triggers me to switch on the ceiling lamps. Time is passing as I'm searching. I should have started a countdown on my phone as a constant reminder of how long I have left to complete my mission. It's not as though I'm slacking at all, but I need to remember, every step I take, that I'm working to a time limit here. I thought of it as three days, but really, I only ever had around 48 hours. I arrived early-afternoon Saturday and Michelle will return around the same time on Monday. Two nights; one full and two half-days. I tricked my own mind from the start.

On paper, I should be able to search the entire house in that time.

Paper, paper, paper.

I'm sick of the word already.

Taking a long, deep breath, I refocus my thoughts. I have to keep searching, and the next place I'm going to look is Michelle Crane's bedroom.

As I make my way upstairs, I can't help but thinking that her door is going to be locked, that there's no way she would leave every area of her home so woefully unguarded – especially if what I am looking for is within the walls of her bedchamber. Up the staircase, onto the landing, and past my own room, I walk, heart in my mouth, the tension almost overwhelming.

When I reach the door to Michelle's room, I stop. I've come into her house, I've rifled through her office, scoured her living room, and whilst that felt wrong, of course it felt wrong, here, now, standing in front of the entrance to her most personal space, I can hardly bring myself to proceed. There's something about a bedroom that demands sanctity and respect. I never go into house owners' personal sleeping spaces unless that's the area they've allocated for me to stay in while they are away. Not everyone has five guest rooms, after all.

Gloves on, I put my hand on the doorknob. It's smooth, polished wood, cold, and I imagine impossibly expensive. The designer of Michelle's home has considered every possible detail. There's no sign of a lock unless it's integral to the opening mechanism. If I turn it, it will open. If I push the door, I'll be inside Michelle Crane's bedroom.

An invisible, imaginary barrier stops me from moving forward.

"I'm sorry," I say, aloud. But there is no one to hear me apart from myself, and I'm in no place to grant forgiveness for my actions.

I don't want to do this.

I really don't want to do this.

But I have to.

I turn the handle and tentatively step inside.

As I cautiously enter Michelle Crane's bedroom, a wave of unease washes over me. The air hangs heavy with anticipation. It's dark in here. The sun has long since set now, and there is only dim light filtering through Michelle's partially closed curtains, casting eerie shadows across the space. I could definitely have done without the effect that this creates. My nerves are already on edge. All it would take is a shift in the lighting to tip me over.

Calm down, I tell myself. *Focus.*

I have to focus.

I stand still, letting my eyes adjust to the darkness. I might be the only person in the house, but I can't shake the feeling that I'm being watched. Hester must have gone home after I saw her earlier. The gates opened to allow her to leave and closed behind her. I can't help but imagine that she could be outside, watching the house for signs that I am up to no good.

It's easy to be paranoid when you're doing something hideously awful.

Get a grip, I think.

Rather than switch on the lights, I pull out my phone and use the torch function. Better to be safe. I can't risk being caught.

Illuminating the area before me, I move with a purpose, my eyes scanning the room for any sign of personal documents, or where they may be stashed.

I thought that my guest room was spacious, but Michelle's sleeping area is twice the size, spanning the entire width of the house. There are windows on two sides of the room, and a doorway in the third wall that I assume leads to her personal bathroom. Her bed appears to be larger than a standard king size, but it is still dwarfed by the room's area. Even though I am here for a nefarious reason, I can't help but have a fleeting awed thought as I cast my eyes around – and shine my torch over – the place that Michelle Crane sleeps.

I shake my head; this is no time to be a fangirl.

I wish I could have taken this assignment under different circumstances. What an opportunity it would have been to house-sit under genuine terms instead of the evil, dishonest way that I have found myself here.

With trembling hands, I began my meticulous search. I have to focus on being systematic. I can't allow knowing that I am an intruder in the very heart of Michelle's private life to distract me from what I have to do. Somewhere amidst the mundane, everyday items could lie the key to unravelling her secrets. The key to regaining my own personal security and safety.

I methodically open drawers, revealing neatly arranged piles of clothes. I have to reach down, underneath the sweaters, slide my hand through each pile in case the documents are sequestered between them. I repeat the process with her trousers, tops and in each of the other drawers. When I come to her lingerie, I pause again, once more distracted by the thought that I am invading Michelle's personal space. Ridiculous considering my motives, but inbuilt within my psyche, that overriding thought that I shouldn't be here. I shouldn't be doing this.

Any other time, I wouldn't be.

Without the threat to my own security, I would never do this.

Focus, I think, and I carry on.

With each passing minute, I delve deeper into Michelle's personal realm, a world she must have thought was hidden away from prying eyes. Day-by-day she invites people to look at her public persona, but here, in her bedroom, this is supposed to be private.

I have to find those documents, and I hope with every beat of my pounding heart that the secrets are kept within the confines of Michelle's bedroom. In this room could lie the key to my safety – and Michelle's downfall.

SEVENTEEN

The carpet in Michelle's bedroom is a thick pile grey wool. As I root through her lower drawers, I put my phone down to illuminate my way, and sit on the floor. Even from this viewpoint, the room is luxurious. I dip my hand into the lace, silk and cottons of her underwear collection – all of it in the same neutral colours that I am so used to seeing her wearing on the outer layers of her clothing. I catch sight of some of the labels that adorn the pants and know without question that each item on its own cost more than I've ever spent on my entire underwear collection.

Sifting through Michelle's most intimate clothing is one step further into the realms of indecency. I hate myself for doing this, and the guilt that I feel for invading Michelle's personal space is unbearable. Still, the stakes are too high for me to have any other option. With each moment that passes, the self-reproach grows, the urgency to find what I am looking for increases, and the tension that this inner conflict is wreaking intensifies.

I try my best to be respectful, but that in itself seems an oxymoron when my hands are deep in Michelle Crane's lingerie. It's impossible to be considerate whilst tapping away at the bottom of the drawer, trying to find out if there's a hidden compartment that could maybe, just maybe, hold the key to my freedom.

This is not the first time that I've felt the deep darkness of shame in my actions. I've made bad decisions in the past – decisions that have led to this situation that I am stuck in today. If I had led a blameless life, there would be nothing to hold over me, nothing to use against me. Though I can't shoulder the responsibility entirely for what I have done, I know the repercussions are my own fault. I have to be accountable for my choices – including the fact that I am here, in Michelle Crane's home, today.

I would love to claim that what I am doing will bring about some kind of redemption for the mistakes of my past, but that's not the case at all. When I deliver Michelle's identity to my caller — my blackmailer — all it will do is prevent my own secrets from being shared.

It's not a temporary measure. I wouldn't be going to these lengths if I thought that someone else could come along and find out the same information about me that my caller did. I was careless; naïve perhaps. I didn't cover my tracks well enough. I left my own personal data where it could be too easily found and used against me – and now I hope that Michelle has made the same mistake. I've cleaned up all my breadcrumbs now. There are no trails leading back into the deep darkness of my past.

Once I find Michelle's documents, I will truly be free.

But at what cost?

I shove my conscience to the recesses of my thoughts and push again at the base of the drawer. I don't want to break it, but a niggling feeling inside me tells me to persist. It doesn't budge.

Kneeling on the floor in front of the unit, I put my hands to either side of the drawer and tilt it up gently, rocking it slightly, to shift it on its casters. It slides out of place easily, and within a few seconds I am holding the drawerful of underwear like a market trader looking for a buyer. I put it down carefully on the carpet beside me, praying that it won't leave a mark, and stare into the dark hole that its absence has created.

Time stops.

The room fades around me.

All I can see is the large box file that is concealed in the space at the bottom of the unit.

An involuntary sound squeaks from my mouth, and I have to put my hands down onto the floor beside me to steady myself as the world shifts into a dizzy haze.

It can't be, but it must be.

This has to be what I am looking for.

I give myself a moment to recover and then reach into the hole and pull out the container. The box is a pale oatmeal shade, although I'm sure that Crane's creative team have thought of a much more aesthetic name for the colour.

There in the bottom right corner is that origami crane logo. I'm not sure that I'll be able to look at that bird again after I leave this place. I'll probably have nightmares about it pecking my eyes out. I can't say that I'd blame it.

The lid is closed with a simple push button on the side. No locks, no security.

Michelle's voice echoes in my head.

You are the security system.

I'm both relieved and repulsed at the same time, and it's not a pleasant combination.

The first thing I see when I pop open the box, right on top of the pile of alligator-clipped statements, is Michelle's birth certificate.

Michelle Andrea Crane.

Date of birth.

Place of birth.

Parents' names.

Serial number.

Original copy.

Everything about this document appears completely genuine.

I can barely breathe as I sift through the papers. Her home utility bills, bank statements for this financial year, the registration document for the car the Hester drove her away in just hours ago.

Everything I need, neatly parcelled up in one place.

My fingers come to a stop as that thought hits me.

All this personal information, printed out, packaged neatly, and kept together? It seems far too convenient. My euphoria at finding the documents is tainted by distrust.

Either Michelle Crane is nowhere near as intelligent as I thought she was, or someone put this pile of documents here for me to find.

I'm being paranoid again; I must be. My caller, my dear caller, told me that the paperwork was here for me to find. They were quite sure that I'd be able to lay my hands on what they needed, so they must have known that Michelle was slapdash about security. Or they have someone on the inside.

I shake my head, trying to dislodge the thought. Just because I am a duplicitous bitch doesn't mean that I can tar anyone else with the same brush. It would be madness to think that Hester (because that, of course, is who my brain is trying to suggest) would have anything to do with betraying Michelle. She would have no reason to do something so divisive.

But what do I know?

It's hardly as though I ran a background check on Michelle's personal assistant before I took this job; I didn't know she existed. Even if I had, there was no way that anything I learned about Hester could have stopped me from coming here. But if Hester were to be in on the whole identity theft, wouldn't my caller have told me? Wouldn't it have been sensible to make my task here just a little easier? Maybe my caller enjoys the game as much as the outcome.

I don't know what to think.

EIGHTEEN

Libby

I make my plan.

I finish the job at Maynard Brookes, give my standard launch presentation and bid a not-at-all-tearful farewell to Amy and the other girls.

On the surface, everything is as it always is: I get home on time, my wages are paid into our joint account at the end of the month, I move on to another company within a few days of completing at Maynard Brookes.

On the surface, nothing has changed.

But only a few weeks after writing out my problems on my notepad, I've already started to put my personal plan into action. It didn't even take a lot of effort on my part; I should have thought of this a long time ago. Instead, I put up and shut up. I tolerated his treatment for far too long. If it wasn't for Amy and her friends, perhaps I would have carried on burying my head in the sand. Making my comfort zone uncomfortable was probably one of the best things that could have happened to me.

I opened another bank account. That was the first part of my plan. I needed a little help with that because I couldn't risk him finding out what I was doing. If he knew I was going behind his back, I didn't know what he was capable of. I spent all my time with him toeing the line, watching my every step, and still he found reasons to punish me. If he uncovered my separate account, the consequences were unimaginable.

The thing about working in a lot of different companies is that even without being able to be a social butterfly, you make business contacts. Sometimes I needed help to grease the wheels and *get things done*. And I mean in the not-quite-legit way. There were a couple of people that I thought might be able to help me without asking too many questions, and I got in touch with one of them, always from work, never from home. Never anywhere that he could trace what I was doing.

I opened another bank account, one that couldn't be traced to me, but that I could use to pay money in, and, when I had saved up enough to get away, that I could withdraw my money from. My money. All the money that I earned was mine, of course, but I wasn't greedy. I couldn't afford to be. I calculated how much I needed, tapping the numbers into those little cells on the spreadsheets that I love so much, and spread that figure over six months. Six months. That's how long I gave myself to save up and be free. That was the additional time that I sentenced myself to. At least I knew that at the end of that period, I would be free.

Or at least that's what I thought.

The extra money had to come from somewhere, of course. He would notice if I suddenly started getting less money than I was supposed to. He kept track of every penny, and the amount that I needed to syphon into my second account would have set off all kinds of alarm bells. I couldn't risk that.

The solution was actually quite obvious. I upped my hourly rate. For someone on minimum wage, a small pay rise would potentially have little impact. However, for someone like me, an expert in their field, out-performing competitors and producing the kind of outcomes that companies were clamouring to hire me for, it was easy to bump up my salary. I upped it by ten per cent and then asked for a retainer at the start of my next contract that would be equal to the increase. That initial fee went straight into my personal account.

As far as Neil would know, I was earning the same as I had been. I knew I could command the increased payment. As worthless as I felt at home, I knew my worth in the workplace, regardless of how my co-workers might treat me.

After three months at an accountancy firm and another quarter in a stationery company, my bank balance had reached the target figure. I finally had the financial means to get away. All I had to do was to find the balls to do it.

NINETEEN

Jude

I slide the drawer back into the pedestal, my hands shaking as I realign it and push it into place. My mind is racing with so many questions. I made a mistake in not thinking through what I was doing here. The task at hand was all that I focused on; I never stopped to consider who was forcing me to do this or why.

Does it really matter?

The end result for me is the same: deliver the papers, avoid having my secrets revealed.

I can't help but keep circling through the same thoughts, though. How did my caller know I would find those papers here, in Michelle's home? Why were the documents I needed packaged so conveniently? They may as well have been inside an envelope with my name on it. *Here you go, Jude, help yourself.*

There's something more significant in motion here. If I'm safe now, though, should I even dig deeper into what that is?

I cast a swift look around Michelle's sleek but opulent bedroom for one last time, checking that nothing shows signs of disturbance, and then make my way back to my bedroom. It may not be my actual room, but while I am here, it's my place of personal privacy. I'm alone in the house, but somehow it feels safer to return there to make my call.

Although I was pleased before that none of the interior rooms have locks, when I get to my room and close the door, I wish I could bolt it behind me. Even though there's no one else in the house, I want to be sealed away. I want to be safe here. I want to be sure.

I have what I came to Michelle's house for, and I need to be certain that I keep hold of these documents until I can pass them over to my caller. I set them down onto the bed, slip off my cotton gloves, and pull my phone from my pocket.

My heart is pounding out of my chest as I click to unlock my phone. I need to take a moment. I've never dialled their number before, it's always them that has been the caller. Now the onus is on me to make the call. I need to pull myself together, stay calm, finish the job.

I slump onto the floor at the side of the bed before clicking the buttons.

It's almost over.

At the other end of the line, the call rings out, and I wait, heart pounding, for them to answer.

It rings.

And rings.

And rings.

Until it stops ringing.

There's no answer.

I've built myself up to this moment that I'm like a coiled spring, ready to snap. The last thing I expected was that my caller wouldn't answer.

I have the papers. I've kept my end of the deal. I need to know that I can deliver them, and that my caller will keep their side of our bargain too.

Before I can relax, I need to know that I am safe.

I stare at the phone, willing it to ring, the voice in my head uttering a silent prayer.

Ring.

I've never wanted to see their number on my screen before. Every time, I've had that gut wrench feeling. Now, though. Now I need closure. I need to know this is over.

Ring.

Please ring.

The phone remains obstinately silent.

I want to throw my useless handset across the room, but I hold back. There's no point letting my emotions take over. I've done what I came to do. They will call, and I will give them the good news. The clock on my phone face tells me it's past ten. I should take the rest of the night to relax, turn on the state-of-the-art television and curl up on the sofa with a glass of the most expensive looking wine I can see in Crane's collection. Because why not?

Despite being sure that I closed the door, I give a swift look in its direction before turning back to the papers onto my bed. I spread them out like a detective in one of those corny movies, looking over each in turn. Michelle's birth certificate. Bank statements for her personal account. Her health insurance schedule. An astronomical phone bill. Is this enough to steal someone's identity? Is this all it comes down to – these simple pieces of paper? Could it really be so easy for someone to destroy another person's life?

My own paperwork described me as a perfect, trustworthy employee, but that just goes to show that you can't believe everything you read.

I gulp; this is who I have become. If you had asked me six weeks ago whether this was the sort of thing I would ever do, I would have been appalled. Back then, I didn't know how far I would go to save myself. I suppose you never know that until you're put to the test. When it comes down to it, perhaps that survival instinct kicks in for everyone. We do what we have to in order to safeguard our existence, no matter the cost. No matter who else we have to hurt to protect our own interests.

I bundle the papers together, reminding myself to be more careful, more methodical, less slapdash. I need to stay calm. Tapping the edges to tidy the pile, I place the documents at the bottom of my travel bag and cover them over with my clothes. I won't be unpacking. Not now. All I want to do is get out of here.

Securing my own safety was what got me into this situation in the first place. My past decisions were necessary, inescapable at the time. I was desperate, and I thought I was taking the only option available to me. Although I thought at the time that if my secrets surfaced one day, I would deal with them if and when that happened, I didn't put enough consideration into what the ramifications could be. That only became significant when the caller made contact and threatened to shatter my world.

Michelle may have been careless with her paperwork.

Hester may be working against her boss.

My caller might know more than I ever considered.

One thing I know for certain: I'm a cog in a far grander machine.

Until my caller contacts me again, there's nothing more I can do.

TWENTY

I spend the evening trying to relax, but I can't bring myself to open the wine. I've done enough damage. Guilt steers me towards a bottle of Tanqueray and a chilled can of tonic from the selection of mixers that Michelle has left in the fridge. I pour myself a double measure, and down it, topping up before adding the mixer to my second helping.

My nerves are shot, and there's no word from my caller.

I try to settle in front of the television, but instead sit scrolling mindlessly through the countless channels, only partly taking in the offerings. There's nothing I want to watch, nothing that can take my mind off the limbo that I dangle in.

When it gets to eleven o'clock and there's still no call, I steel myself to try dialling again. It feels so alien to be the caller, but I don't know if I'll sleep without having made contact.

I thought that they would have been as eager as I was to get their hands on the documents. I'm sure it's too late now, at this time of night, for them to come and collect the papers. As I contemplate this, it strikes me that I don't exactly know what the procedure for exchange will be. I give them the documents and they give me their word: that's all I have. I suppose once they have Michelle's identification details and use them for whatever nefarious purposes they intend, I will also know *their* secret. I will know what they have done.

In truth, I know nothing at all about my caller.

I don't have a name for them; I don't know where they are; I don't even know their gender. From the outset they have used voice distortion every time we have spoken. I did consider that this might be the reason that they couldn't, or wouldn't, answer my call to them – they weren't prepared to speak to me. I should have picked up on the voice manipulation the first time they called me, but with the storm going on around me I couldn't hear as clearly as usual. Something seemed awry, but when my caller began to make their demands, I was side-tracked, distracted by the more immediate danger.

Because of what the caller knows about me, I assumed them to be a man. The kind of information that they have on me doesn't simply fall into the hands of a woman. I don't know when or how they found out about my past, but they know enough to cause me a lot of trouble. I doubt I could continue working as a house sitter if my background were to be made available to prospective clients. What I didn't stop to think about, when the caller first threatened me, was that it's highly unlikely that I'll be able to carry on working in this job if I'm found out as a thief.

I have no motive to steal from Michelle. There's nothing that could connect me to my caller. I have a spotless track record. I'm covering my tracks in the house impeccably.

Still, now I have the documents, I want to hand them over and be done with this. Monday afternoon, and my exit from this house can't come quickly enough.

Only a few weeks ago, when I sat in the storm blown Dorset cottage and spoke to my caller for the first time, they told me what they wanted from me, and gave me all kinds of reassurances that what I was about to do would never come back to damn me.

"There's no danger of any kind of recrimination, dear," the voice said.

My mind was still spinning, trying to get to grips with the fact that someone had found out about my not-so-perfect past. I thought I had covered my tracks, I thought there was no evidence left of what I had done. What had I missed? How had I been so stupid?

"How can you be so sure?" I stopped questioning myself and started asking the things I needed to know. "If there's only me in the house and things go missing…"

"I'm going to deal with that," the disguised voice replied.

The gale thrashed the windows, and the more timid of the cats, Diana, leapt up onto the seat beside me, insinuating herself into my orbit. I switched my phone to the opposite hand, and petted her, feeling the damp of her fur against my slowly warming palm. It was my duty to stay in the homes of others and protect not only their house, but the things inside it that they held dear. I wouldn't have dreamt of harming the sweet cat that purred and pressed itself against me as I listened to the voice at the other end of the phone continue. How could I consider searching for personal, private paperwork that could cause serious damage to a stranger? A stranger who was trusting me, at that.

"And if I say no…" I let the statement trail off and form a question.

"Well, Jude dear," the voice said. Although disguised, I could still pick up the malevolent tone. "I believe that you're going to find your own little life crumbling down around your feet."

"How do I know you have anything on me at all?" I knew already, as I spoke the words, that my response to the caller's threats meant that there was no way that I could deny any wrongdoing. If I had thought more quickly, perhaps I could have claimed they had the wrong number, the wrong person, that I, Judith Quinn, had never put a step out of line, and that there was nothing they could know and use against me. I was taken aback, though, by the phone call, by the coercive demands, by the very fact that someone had found me out, and then had actually found me.

It was too late to roll back and respond differently to the conversation.

I sat, stroking Diana with a trembling hand, waiting for a reply. There was the sound of muffled movement at the other end of the line, and then a loud triple beep sounded out from my phone, sending the cat scuttling back across the room to the other chair.

A text message.

A photograph.

Another.

A third.

All the evidence I needed to show that my caller did indeed know about my past, and could corroborate what I had done.

Shit.

I couldn't look at the photo messages, I didn't want to see the person I used to be for a second longer than necessary. I wasn't that person anymore. I couldn't relate to how I was, who I was, or what I had done. All I wanted – all I want now – was to leave that behind me and move on with my life.

I thought that's what I was doing.

"So you see, Jude, my dear, you've left yourself open for a little, how shall I put it?" The harshness in the caller's voice was replaced by bitter saccharine sweetness.

"Blackmail," I replied, deadpan.

"Negotiation?" the voice offered, with a droll laugh.

"I don't do this for you, and I'm screwed. I do this and I'm screwed. Sensitive documents go missing while I'm house-sitting? There's only one person they're going to point the finger at."

"You would think so, wouldn't you?" my caller replied. "But the thing is, and this is the case for a lot of people who have more money than sense, when you have something that can damage someone else, you can manipulate that person. You can control them. You can get them to do things they wouldn't normally ever imagine that they could do. You can stop them from doing things that they really think they should do. Michelle Crane is a woman with many secrets. You don't need to know about them. All you need to know is that there are documents I need, they are in her house, and you are going to get them for me."

It's only when the caller stopped speaking that I realised how rapid and laboured my breathing had become. I've never had a panic attack, but it felt like I was going to slip into something very close to that.

"Take a breath, why don't you?" the voice said, dispassionately, and I took the advice.

Lightning flared, and I braced for another round of rolling thunder. By my side now, Camilla and Diana were lying so close together that they formed an indistinguishable black furry mound; impossible to determine where one cat ended, and the other began. If I had someone, anyone, to turn to, perhaps there might have been a way out of the nightmare situation. But I was alone, I am alone, and I knew there was no way that I could avoid what was to come.

The booming roar reverberated, and I tried, tried, tried to calm myself.

"You'll do it?" That time, the question could only be interpreted as a statement.

"I don't have a choice," I said.

I don't know if I expected them to reply with a glib 'of course you do'. If they had told me that, it would have been a lie.

"I'll be in touch," the voice said, and the phone clicked to silence.

I was alone with the building storm.

That night, I pulled my duvet down into the living room and curled up on the chaise, just as my feline companions had settled on the other sofa. I couldn't bear to go upstairs into the homeowners' bed. I felt dirty, even though the darkness of what I had to do was still ahead of me.

Now, in Michelle's home, with its five opulent bedrooms and luxurious beds, I find myself again unable to take my place upstairs. I would sully everything I touched, and this place, this entire house is too good for me. Instead, I pull a cream cashmere throw over me, and with my phone still in my hand, lay my head on the arm of the sofa, sliding into undeserved sleep.

TWENTY-ONE

Unexpectedly, I sleep deeply.

With everything that has happened during my stay at the Crane house, I didn't imagine that I would be able to settle, but perhaps nervous exhaustion could account for the full nine hours that I manage to pass on the sofa.

I might have even managed longer, but I am awoken by a clicking sound in the atrium and the clacking of heels across the marble floor.

"Michelle?" I call out, in my semi-awake state.

"Sorry to disappoint," Hester says, as she walks into the living room. "Only me."

"Not at all," I say, pulling myself upwards, into a sitting position and frantically straightening my hair with my fingers.

"Don't bother with that," Hester gestures. "No photoshoots today."

I wonder if she says the same to Michelle when she sees her in the mornings. There are photographs of some kind every day for Crane, professional or personal.

I can't stop myself from turning beetroot red. I don't know what to say. All I can think of is a lame '*good morning*'.

"Uh-huh, good morning," she says, looking at her Apple watch. "It is still morning, just about."

She sits down on the velvet sofa and looks at me quizzically. I feel as though I am being examined, somehow. It could just be the guilt of knowing that Michelle's paperwork is at the bottom of my travel bag. My heart skips a beat with the relief that I managed to stash the papers in my holdall rather than leaving them out on the bed. What if she had gone straight upstairs and found them laying there?

Act naturally, I tell myself. *Be cool*.

"Just about," I say, trying to inject a friendly edge rather than let her hear how irritated I am by her presence. "I was so tired last night. I must have passed out down here." Then I pause before asking, "Did you need something?"

Hester lets out a small chuckle.

"I usually come over mid-morning on a Sunday. It's my lying day."

"Lying?" I repeat, confused.

"Lie-in," she says, stretching the words. Did I mishear or is she having fun at my expense.

I choose to laugh it off. "Me too," I say.

"Michelle has great coffee, if you want to make some," she says, with the implication that she would like some too. I'm sure if I were Michelle, Hester would have brewed fresh and brought it up to me in my bedroom along with homemade waffles or whatever it is that looks Sunday-morning social media worthy. If I were Michelle, I probably wouldn't have crashed on the sofa.

"Uh, sure," I say. Perhaps coffee isn't a bad idea. I don't need the caffeine jolt, the adrenaline buzzing through me is quite enough tension, but I need to wake up, get my head in the game, and sharpen my focus. "Can I get you one?"

"Black, please. No sugar."

I can't help but think it would have been easier for her to make the drinks, seeing as she knows where everything is kept, and how she likes her own brewed, but it's clear that there is a power play at work here. Hester is always Michelle's underling, following her around and standing on the side-lines. Now I'm the paid help. It must be satisfying for her to have someone to talk down to. I'm a nobody. I'm worse than a nobody.

I find the coffee machine and kick it into motion.

All I can think about as the beans brew is how much I need Hester to leave so that I can contact my caller and draw this whole shitshow to a close.

I take a sip from my expensive-looking mocha-glazed cup before carrying the two drinks back through into the living room.

Hester has settled back onto the sofa, so calm in her surroundings that it's almost as though this is her house and not Michelle's. If I didn't know who Crane was and I was invited into this home, I could easily mistake Hester for the homeowner. Even though she would never in a thousand years be able to afford a place like this. I wonder where she lives, and how on earth Michelle ever ended up with someone like Hester working as her PA. I think I would have chosen someone with more style and definitely with more impressive social skills. As proven through her choice of house sitter, though, Michelle is capable of making poor decisions.

"Are you here for something in particular today?" I ask, as Hester drinks a little of her coffee and scowls. "Or did you just fancy a chat?"

I'm trying to keep it light, but I want to get to the point. I need to know why she is here, and I want her to leave. My caller could get in contact with me at any time, and they are going to want confirmation that I have completed my task. I can't wait to tell them. I can't wait for this to be over.

"Yes, actually," Hester says, flatly. "You see, I don't know much about you, Jude."

I wouldn't expect her to. I don't know much about her either. Only yesterday evening, I was wondering whether she was in on the plot to dethrone her employer. That seems like such a fanciful idea in the cold light of day.

I can understand her caution. I'm a hired house sitter. All she or Michelle knows about me is what it says on my profile and in my references.

I shrug and fake a smile.

"I know Michelle trusts those *Homesitter* people," she says, leaning towards me. "We've had girls from there before," she says, placing emphasis on the word 'girls' even though I'm clearly an adult woman. Something about the way she says it riles me. Instead of reacting, though, I force myself to remain impassive and refuse to give her the reaction she no doubt wants.

"But I like to do a little background reading," she says.

There's nothing to find, I tell myself. *Everything is fine.*

I can't help but feel a shard of guilt jabbing into my conscience, though.

I can't let it show.

I listen as she continues.

"The problem is this. I went to look you up. And do you know what I found out?"

I shake my head.

"Not a lot, I would think. I'm not a very interesting person, I'm afraid." I'm about to add a little quip about how not all of us can be jetsetters like Michelle, but instead I decide that less is more, and I keep my mouth shut.

"I found nothing," Hester says, flopping back onto the sofa.

I feel relief wash over me. It lasts a split second, because I can see on Hester's face that she's not happy with the results of her search.

"Right," I say, still keeping my emotions in check.

"There's nobody these days that doesn't have some kind of internet presence. Even if you don't have an Instagram account or keep in touch with those old school friends on Facebook that you haven't seen for fifteen years and will probably never see again. Even if your careers advisor hasn't talked you into setting up a LinkedIn profile. Even if, even if… it's rare to find anyone with no kind of social footprint."

I'm about to speak, to tell her I have private accounts and don't post anything; it's true. She raises a hand to silence me and carries on.

"But, when I typed JUDE QUINN into the search box, I didn't get anything in return. Or at least I didn't get anything related to this mousy little woman…" She waves her hand generally in my direction as she says this, "…who is staying at Michelle Crane's home right now. It's almost as though…" Hester pauses, cocking her head to the side. "...she doesn't exist."

All the time that Hester is unleashing her words, I'm trying to decide how to play this. I could laugh it off. *Of course I exist, I'm here.* I could try to justify myself. *I'm not really into social media.* What I can't do is tell the truth, or at least not the entire truth.

"No Jude Quinn. No Judith Quinn." Hester looks at me, much as an enemy might watch someone who had slipped from a ledge and was clinging on by their fingertips for dear life. Curious interest; waiting for me to fall to my death.

"Yeah," I say, eventually, as casually as I can manage. "I didn't really want to be found."

Hester doesn't move, and barely responds. There's just a slight raise of her eyebrows, as she waits for me to say more. I don't want to, but I'm afraid that I can't hang on for much longer. I have to give her something or she's probably going to push me down rather than help me up.

"Relationship stuff." I condense an excruciating period of misery into two words, as if it were nothing. Brush it off, bat it away. It's in the past now, all of that is behind me, everything I've done in my life is behind me.

161

Or at least it will be when I have delivered Michelle Crane's secrets.

"How awful," Hester says with such a lack of emotion that I can tell she couldn't care less about my dating history. Perhaps she's simply disappointed that there could be such a straightforward explanation for my lack of online presence.

The best lies are those that are part-truths.

TWENTY-TWO

Libby

The next part of my plan is more difficult. I don't just want to get away from Neil, I want to make sure he can't find me. I want to be sure that he can never hurt me again.

My LinkedIn profile tracks my every job move, and I need to keep it current to continue to secure the kind of assignments that will allow me to carry on working and earning money. I know, though, that when I leave Neil, I'm going to have to cover my tracks. Sure, companies could contact me directly, but that would mean making my details public – and he could contact me too.

Work has been my safe haven for so long, but that was when I had needed it to be. I have needed the high income to support my unemployed husband and myself. With only one person to think about, perhaps I can get by dialling it down, switching to a different line of work, changing lanes to somewhere that Neil will never be able to find me.

When I first had that thought, it terrified me. Project management is all I've ever known. I went to university and then took a bunch of short courses to skill me up in particular approaches and techniques. All my eggs have been in a single basket, and it feels like I'm about to crack every one of them.

The initial fear subsided, and I went through a short period of being angry that I was going to have to leave a field where I was an expert, just to get away from him. I haven't done anything wrong. I haven't done anything to deserve the situation that I am in. Why should I have to give up *anything*? I already have to leave the home that I love. I've never once felt any sadness about leaving the man that I loved, because Neil is so far from the person who I fell in love with that he's barely recognisable to me now.

Have I let him down somehow? Could I have prevented his downward spiral and metamorphosis into the sour, spiteful man he has become? Was any of this my fault? I know I can't let myself think this way.

Things are what they are. I have to deal with the situation that I am in, to the best of my ability. It's time to get my head down and get on with it. If I wanted to be sure that he can't find me, I have to do everything I can to become untraceable.

I need to become a different person.

I choose the day carefully. It's a Monday; the first day of the week; the first day of my new life. On Friday I delivered my end of project report to the manager at the stationery company and received the final payment into my bank account. I could have left earlier when I had the money paid into my *secret* account. It would have been easy to skip town, walk out there and then, and never look back. But they had paid me the retainer for the work they expected me to do, and I'm not the kind of person who would defraud anyone else like that. Even though it meant staying with Neil, going through the heightening level of abuse for three more months, I owed it to Libby Halstead, to the person I was, the person I was leaving behind, to leave her with dignity.

So, I completed the project, and today, a warm Monday at the beginning of Spring, I start my new life.

I'm finally leaving.

Neil murmurs beside me as the alarm goes off. Half past seven. I wake up at the same time every day, regardless of where I'm working. I don't take any jobs that would entail a commute of longer than an hour. Neil expects me home by six o'clock, dinner on the table by six forty-five. My routine has been set in stone, but today that all changes.

As usual, when I silence the bleeping from my phone, Neil rolls over, moving away from me, settling back to sleep. He'll probably lie-in until midday, and by then, I'll be gone. Of course, he won't realise that until five past six this evening, and by then it will be too late. Libby Halstead will no longer exist.

At this point in the day, I usually drag myself to the bathroom without delay, brush my hair, do my make-up. I have to shower at night, because it wakes Neil up when I do it in the morning. It's too loud for him, too inconvenient for me to get ready for work the way I want to. That was never the case when he was working. We would shuffle around the bathroom together each day, him shaving while I took my shower. On more than one occasion, he came in to join me and make us both late for work with his spontaneity. The thought of that, and how I once felt about our physical intimacy, before it was something that I endured instead of enjoyed, makes me stop to look over at my almost-sleeping husband.

It wasn't always like this.

But if I stay, it will never change.

At least not for the better.

I've packed only one bag. I know he won't notice. He pays no attention to what I take to work with me. Today I'm taking what I need for a quick getaway. Without turning around to look at what I am leaving behind, I walk out of the door. There's an e-ticket, whatever that is, on the train app on my phone, and a flat waiting for me at the other end of the line. I've had six months to plan. I'm ready.

I could have taken the car with me. It's the most expensive thing I've ever owned, apart from the house, but logic told me it was traceable, that if I had the car with me, it would form part of a paper trail, potentially leading him to my new door. When I thought about how hard I worked to buy my Tesla, it was near impossible to bring myself to leave it.

But it was metal, plastic and rubber, and not worth risking my safety for.

I told Neil, when I bought it, that it was a necessity, that I needed a status symbol to show what a successful, desirable project manager I was. That was a lie. I find displays of wealth like that vulgar, and even though the real reason gave me cause to smile, driving around in that car left a sour taste in my mouth. And the real reason? I wanted – finally – to spend at least some of the money that I had earned. Everything I had went into our joint account, and I had nothing to show for the hours of hard work, overtime, and back-to-back assignments that left me with no holidays, no opportunity to wind down and decompress. Nothing for myself.

The lack of holidays was actually a benefit. No time off meant that I wasn't stuck in the house with him any longer than I had to be. When we both worked, I would look forward to the annual leave he booked, and I'd make sure that I wasn't on assignment when he took his vacation days. That seems such a long time ago that I can't remember what it felt like to want to be with him.

The person Neil was back then would never have said the things to me that he did in the long years between lockdown and when I left him. The old Neil would never have physically hurt me; I don't think he would ever have even imagined he could become the person that he did. I know I couldn't have. But maybe that part of him was always there, simmering under the surface. Perhaps it was inevitable that my career would skyrocket, leaving him on the launch pad, watching through his green, jealous eyes as I flew into orbit.

If it had been the other way around, I would have cheered from the ground as he soared. Most of the time I felt as though he wanted to see me circle close to the sun and spiral back to earth. That wasn't true, though. Envious as he was, he wanted me to succeed, but only because it meant that he could stay at home, live off my money, and keep me under his control.

But when you've learnt how to fly, someone can only keep you grounded for so long. By the time I had saved enough money to leave, my wings were aching to be stretched, and if I had to leave the nest with nothing, then so be it.

I found a flat, nothing special. I've not got a job lined up. I've spent so many years sliding seamlessly from one company to another that I've assumed that it can't be all that difficult. I'm taking enough money to cover the rent for a few months. I've planned my exit as though I was planning one of the projects that I have been such a specialist at managing.

There's always some allowance for risk, but this time I've miscalculated. I've made assumptions, and whoever said that when you assume it makes an ass out of you and me was bang on the money.

I've messed up. Big time.

TWENTY-THREE

Jude

I don't for one moment think that Hester is satisfied with the answer that I've given her, even though it is based on the truth. I stay off social media, or at least I refrain from posting, because I don't want my private life broadcast to anyone and everyone. My ethos is the opposite of Michelle Crane's. She has built a brand around her own personal image. Paper Crane would be just another stationery company if it wasn't for the high-end feel she has imbued it with by creating her inimitable online persona. She's a smart woman.

The thought hits me again that Crane is far too savvy to leave herself open to exploitation like this. Would someone so self-aware really leave her private paperwork in such an easily accessible place? All bundled together? Would she really leave someone like me with the degree of responsibility and access that she has done?

Guilt, paranoia, and fear have scrambled my thought process. I don't know what to think anymore.

If Hester has come here to interrogate me, perhaps I can ask some questions of my own. I take a breath and lean back against the sofa, trying to make myself look more relaxed than I am feeling.

"How long have you been with Michelle?" I ask. I didn't put much thought into the phrasing, and surprise myself with the way it comes out.

She regards me for a few seconds before replying.

"I've worked for Michelle since, uh…" Hester screws up her face, as if in deep thought. "For about three years now."

"Right," I say, trying to keep the conversation moving. For someone who came over to the house knowing that I was here, she doesn't seem keen to chat. "Have you worked for people like her before?"

"There isn't really anyone like Michelle," Hester says. It's sickly, but I manage a smile. I should at least pretend that I'm impressed by the homeowner. It's not that I'm *not* impressed. Michelle is a fine example of a self-made woman; a 'girl-boss' everyday superhero of sorts. If you're looking for that kind of motivational vibe and want to feel like you too could one day achieve this kind of lifestyle, follow Michelle Crane. Buy her products. Steal her secrets.

Don't do that. Don't do that.

"No," she says, answering the question again. "I haven't. Have you?"

Damn. I wanted to keep the focus on Hester, and here she goes, turning it back around.

"I can't really talk about former clients," I say with the sweetest smile that I can force to my face. "I'm sure you wouldn't want me to talk about Michelle and her house."

Hester lets out a sharp laugh. "I don't think there are many people who haven't seen

Michelle's house. It's all over the internet. You may have noticed."

I nod, taking note of her answer. No trace of any suggestion that she is onto me. It's a risk, but I decide to push further.

"That's the side of Michelle that she wants everyone to see though, surely. All those online images are carefully curated, no doubt? She must take twenty photos for every one that she shares?"

Hester leans forward in the most open gesture that I've seen from her so far.

"Let me tell you something," she says. "I've seen Michelle throw on her own make-up, run a brush through her hair and take a stream of perfect photographs. Every single one of them share-worthy. Every single one would get her a hundred thousand likes, hearts, thumbs up, whatever it is they're doing these days. Every single one would make people buy her products."

"Must be nice," I laugh, trying to make it sound natural, trying to bring Hester further out of her professional shell and closer to wanting to open up to me.

She snorts and leans back, away from me again.

"I'm sure it must," she says. Her tone makes me think that she's reconsidering how much she ought to be saying about her employer. There's a renewed guardedness about her.

Hester's eyes drift out to the garden, and I follow her gaze. It's shaping up to be a warm day. Perhaps once I've spoken to my caller, I can get outside, try to unwind in the gardens. I don't want to stay in this house a moment longer than I have to.

Thinking about my caller is enough to increase my pulse rate and send my brain spiralling back into the darkness.

I can't think about them now.

Be calm. Focus.

Although I don't deserve any good luck, I find some, as Hester is too busy looking out of the window to spot my moment of panic.

"Can I ask you something?" It's the kind of question that is always answered with a positive response.

"Sure," Hester says, turning back to me. "Why not?"

"Okay. Uh, why does Michelle hire house sitters? I mean, why doesn't she ask you to stay here while she is away?"

Hester pouts slightly.

"I have a room here," she says.

It's news to me. Even though I haven't had to search through the other bedrooms, I assumed that each of them was an empty guest suite, like the one I have been allocated. I can't even place where this thought has come from. It's as though the house gives off a vibe that I can't place. Everything is perfect, but it feels like an empty, lonely kind of bliss.

"I rarely sleep over. Only when Michelle needs me to." Hester shrugs. "Or on special occasions." With that, she laughs, as though she's just shared a joke that she isn't sharing with me.

"Oh," I say, pretending to be more impressed than I am. "If I had a room here, I would probably never go home."

There's no hint of a smile at that.

"Perhaps Michelle will like you enough to let you stay," Hester says. There's a strange sneer to her voice, as though she knows Michelle would do nothing of the sort, and that I am out of her and Michelle's league. She wouldn't be wrong.

Hester didn't exactly answer my question, I note.

There's just something about the whole situation that is niggling away at me. I feel like if I enquired in the right way, I might find out what it is, but I'm at a loss. I don't want to bring attention to myself and what I'm doing here, but I wish there was a way that I could reassure myself that Hester is not involved. From what she has said, I believe she is loyal to Michelle, but from what I have said, she probably thinks the same about me.

The thing with personality is that if you try hard enough, you can show other people only what you want them to see. Michelle might be able to take one photo and share her glowing, perfect self with the internet-savvy world, but I have to plan carefully what parts of myself to reveal.

Hester would have to dig a lot deeper to uncover my true self, and I really hope that she doesn't manage to do that.

TWENTY-FOUR

Hester hangs around making chit chat way past the point that I lose interest. Still, after she leaves, the house feels like an empty shell. Even though I couldn't wait for her to go, there's something missing without her presence. For a moment, I feel like I can understand why Michelle keeps her personal assistant around. Sure, most of the time Crane is living her high roller lifestyle, travelling, partying and whatever else it is that's currently trending on social media, but when she is here, in her house, there must be times when she gets lonely. I know I would.

I slept for most of the morning and Hester hung around so long that by the time she's left, my stomach is growling for food. I throw some bread into the toaster, and smile as I think about how toast perfectly matches the colour scheme of Crane's home. Everything springs from that neutral palette; her aesthetic is so finely planned that I can't help but wonder if she does make her dietary choices in line with her harmonious environment.

When crumbs fall from the plate as I spread butter on the two slices of sourdough, even they appear to fit in with the tones of the work surface. The more everything appears well-placed and coordinated, the less I feel I should be here. I'm not suited to this house; Michelle should never have chosen me to work for her.

I nibble at the crust, but my thoughts have already turned back to what I have done, what I am doing, and I can't bring myself to eat.

How can I do this to someone else?

How can I gain a position of trust and then let someone down so heinously?

I'm disgusted with myself to the point that I slide the toast into the trash can and wash my hands under the sleek designer tap, all the time shaking my head and cursing beneath my breath.

I have no choice, I know, but this is not me.

The phone remains silent. Why has my caller not made contact to check up on me? I would have thought that they would be eager to know how I am getting on with their nauseatingly vile plan. My bitterness towards whoever it is at the other side of this plot is growing; I can feel it blooming inside of me, second only to my blossoming guilt. Soon I will be filled with the darkness; little black flowers of evil choking the goodness from my heart.

I'm still wearing yesterday's clothes, but the sticky, dirty feeling that I'm carrying runs deeper than my dress. I don't know if I'll ever feel clean again.

A shower seems pointless, but why not give it a try? I make a quick plan to wash and dress, and then call my dear blackmailer again. Not exactly my standard kind of Sunday.

I drop my clothes in a pile on the floor of the en suite and twist the dial until a pleasantly hot waterfall gushes down. The shower is separate from the tub, even in this, my guest room. I never made it into Michelle's bathroom, and as

I step under the downpour, I wonder what luxuries she added for the en suite in her own room. I would have a jacuzzi, perhaps. The kind of bubbles I've only experienced one time in my life, when I was…

My thoughts are interrupted by a sound from the stack of clothing on the floor. My phone is ringing.

I step backwards too suddenly and almost lose my footing. I grab hold of the soap dish, thrust my other arm out to the wall and catch my balance just in time.

Leaving the water cascading, I push open the shower door and flap around for my towel.

Of course, they would wait until I was indisposed before calling. Despite being irked by the timing, I can only be grateful that they didn't phone me while Hester was here. I don't think my caller is the type of person who deals well with being sent through to answerphone.

These thoughts pass through my head as I'm wrapping myself in the towel and rummaging through my mass of clothing, trying to get hold of my phone.

My damp hand makes contact, and I wipe off some of the moisture against my discarded dress before clicking to answer the call.

"Hello?" I say, more out of breath than I had expected.

"Have I caught you at a bad time, Jude?"

There will never be a good time, but considering I'm now alone and able to have the conversation that I need to with my caller, it's not terrible.

"I was in the shower," I admit. My hair is dripping down my face. I hadn't had time to wash it before my phone started to ring, but I'd stood under the water long enough to drench it to the scalp. With one hand occupied by my phone, I can only try half-heartedly to mop at my head with the end of the towel.

Despite asking the question, my caller seems disinterested in the answer. Instead, they continue with their own agenda.

"Do you have the documents I asked for?"

"Yes," I say. I don't let any emotion leak into my voice. I can't give them the satisfaction. I take no joy in what I am doing to Michelle Crane. She doesn't deserve this.

"Good." The reply is as flat as my own monosyllabic response. I thought they would be pleased, now that I've done what they sent me here for. There's no excitement in their voice though. "All of them?" they ask.

"Apart from the passport, of course. If you need it, I can…" I haven't thought about how I could get that from Michelle when she will no doubt have it in her bag when she arrives home, but the offer slips out of my mouth, anyway.

"That won't be necessary. If you have everything else."

I've already said that I do. I want this over.

"So, what now?" I ask. "We make the exchange?"

There's a sharp hitch of breath at the other end of the line, and something that almost sounds like a laugh.

"Well, Jude, my dear. Getting those documents…well, that wasn't exactly *everything* that I wanted from you."

The sentence is long and drawn out, and I have to take a few moments to process what is being said.

"What?" I ask.

"I'm sorry to have wasted your time, Jude, but those documents, well…" I hear a clicking noise, and a deep inhalation before the voice continues. "I don't need them. Not really. Well, I might do, in future. Kind of in the same way that I needed the evidence that I have on you. The documents are a back-up plan. A bartering tool, you could say."

"You're planning to blackmail Michelle Crane too?" I say the words without thinking. Blackmail. I don't think I've dared to accuse my caller of this before, even though that's exactly what's going on here.

"Too?" This time the laugh is clear. "Is that what this is, Jude? I thought we had ourselves a business agreement. You do a job for me, and I…well, you know what I am doing for you. Your dirty little secret is safe with me as long as you keep playing the game, my dear."

"I've done what you asked! I risked everything to get you those documents."

"Then it shouldn't be any trouble for you to find what I really want."

The thought is burning in my mind. I have to say it.

"And then? How do I know that whatever I do for you, you aren't going to keep asking for more and more? How do I know that you're going to stop and leave me the hell alone once I…once I…"

Any chance of me trying to conceal my emotions is far behind me. Hot tears are trailing down my cheeks, and I can't hide the juddering shake in my voice.

"Take a breath, Jude. Sit yourself down. It's okay. Let it out."

The voice is almost believably calming, but I know all they want is to keep using me as a puppet.

I can't do it.

I have to do it.

I gulp in a heavy breath and ask, "What do you want?"

TWENTY-FIVE

Libby

Even though I need to make a clean break from Neil, there's a part of me that wishes I could see his reaction when he realises I'm not coming home. I can't help but wonder what his first emotion will be, whether he would be sad that I was gone, or angry that I haven't come back. If I was a gambling woman, my money would be on the latter; I'm pretty sure the thought that I could get away from him is enough to crush his ego.

I did leave a note, but only because I didn't want him to go to the police, report me as missing, make it even more difficult for me to blend into an anonymous future without him.

> Neil –
> Please don't try to find me.
> I couldn't take it anymore.
> What is here is yours now. And I am not here.
> I hope that in the future you will find happiness and peace.
> I need that for myself too.
> I loved you,
> Libby

I wrote and crossed out words over and over until I realised that short and sweet would work best. They say that less is more, and this time I believed it. Although I know Neil has to take responsibility for the way he has treated me, and what he has done to me, I also know that the person he has become is down to circumstance.

I did love him.

I wish things had been different.

But they are not.

Getting off the train in a new town, using the map app on my new phone (because of course I couldn't risk having him trace me that way) and making my way to a new home gives me a heady mix of excitement and trepidation. I have to go easy on myself. Leaving behind one life and trying to start a new one can't be easy for anyone.

I wish there had been another way.

Not more than fifty meters from the station, the heavens open and torrential rain falls upon me and my solitary bag. I don't have an umbrella, and for a fleeting second, I think about running home to fetch it. It's an instinctive response; the home I am thinking of is two hundred miles away, and it's not my home anymore. Instead, I make the token gesture of pulling up the hood on my sweatshirt and I quicken my pace.

By the time I arrive at the address I've been given – or should it be the address that I've taken? – I'm soaked to the skin. My emotions have swung towards a raw anger at the knowledge that I won't be able to get into my warm bath and soak in my favourite bubbles then dry off with my familiar fluffy towels. I don't even have a towel. That was one thing that I mistakenly thought that I could replace once I was here: give myself a couple of days to get straight and kit out the flat with all the necessities. My savings in the sneaky account will run to the bare minimum. I still don't have a new job to go to.

Tomorrow, I think. *Worry about that tomorrow.*

The key is in a lockbox to the side of the entrance. My frozen fingers fumble the numbers, one dial sticks, refusing to twist to the digit that I have been given, and I curse silently. Everything I had is gone. My creature comforts are behind me in a life to which I can never return. This is all I have now. I have to make it work.

Resolutely, I give the dial a firm shove, and the code clicks into place. If only my life could fall into place as easily.

I hadn't seen the flat before I arrived. I made some excuse to the landlord that I was travelling for a job, and that the virtual tour that the estate agent had posted on their website was enough for me, if he was happy to take me on. I should, perhaps, have taken his eagerness to accept me as a red flag. Who lets a stranger rent out their property without even meeting them? Maybe that happens more often than I think, but it seems now, looking back, that I could have thought about this a little more carefully.

This area of town was described as 'up and coming', which perhaps I could have interpreted as 'currently a shithole'. It's a starting point though. This is just the first page of my new life. I can write the rest of the story for myself. Still, for now, I can't help but notice how run-down and shoddy the flat appears. The carpet on the stairs appears to be new, and as I go up to the first floor, I notice that someone has tried to paint over the graffiti, though I can still make out the words through the low-quality white matt.

On the tiny landing, I pause for a moment, feeling the weight of my bag with everything I now own bearing down on my shoulder. This is it. This is the freedom I wanted.

Whatever lies on the other side of this door is better than the life I was living before.

If I repeat this to myself enough, perhaps I will start to believe it.

I slide the key into the lock and push my way into my new life.

TWENTY-SIX

Jude

Wrapped only in the towel, I have a deep sense of vulnerability as I wait for the caller's reply. I'm still in the steamy bathroom, under the artificial but evidently expensive lighting. It's starting to feel cell-like, so I kick open the door and walk through into the airy bedroom. Still a cell, only bigger. I'm stuck here in this house until I do whatever else it is that the caller wants from me. No matter what it is, I'm not in a position to say no. Not only do they have my past in their pocket, but now they also know that I have stolen from Michelle Crane.

Is it theft if the documents are still in my bag, still in her house? I haven't committed a crime yet, have I? My conscience knows the answer.

"What do you want?" I hiss again, more harshly than I had meant to. I don't have any control in this situation, and I know it. I've got to stay calm. Worst of all, I've got to do what I'm told.

I hear a sharp intake of breath from the other end of the line as though my caller is trying to calm themselves too.

"I'm going to forgive your attitude, my dear," the voice says. "I know this whole situation must be terribly difficult for you. You probably never expected that your wicked past would come back to haunt you like this. I don't suppose you ever considered the implications of your actions, did you?" The voice doesn't pause to let me answer, but I did. I did consider. I made decisions to save myself then, and I am doing exactly the same thing now.

I feel defeated. All I can do is listen.

"Unless you got very lucky, you no doubt searched most of the house for those documents you've found."

I don't take it as a question, so I don't reply at first. When the line remains quiet, I realise, and give a simple confirmation.

"If you've already looked everywhere, you've probably already seen what I *really* want. So you see, dear…" I shudder at the word. "This shouldn't be any trouble at all. Just a tiny little extra job for you. One more thing that I need you to find."

I'm simultaneously irritated and relieved. If there was something else, why didn't they ask for that in the first place? I feel as though they are playing games with me, and considering the dire situation that I'm in, I don't like it one bit.

Still, that hardly matters. If my caller is changing the terms of our agreement, I have to comply. I'm in too deep to do anything else.

"What is it?" I ask, keeping my voice as steady as I can manage. I've curled myself up into a foetal position without even thinking, my towel tightening across my chest, my legs tucked up towards me.

The caller sighs, as though they don't actually want to tell me, and then there's a brief pause. I wait, looking out towards the window and beyond, wishing that I was somewhere, anywhere other than here.

Perhaps not anywhere.

"Well, Jude. I know your secrets, and for us to move forward, unfortunately I need to tell you more about myself. No matter what we try to hide, sometimes we have to reveal a few facts here and there." There's another deep breath from my caller. If this is difficult for them, I can't help but take some pleasure from that fact. "I haven't exactly been honest with you, my dear."

As far as I was aware, they hadn't told me anything about themselves, but I say nothing and listen.

"I actually know Michelle Crane rather well," the voice continues. "Intimately."

At this, I lift my head and shuffle up into a sitting position, tugging at the towel to prevent it from slipping.

"You must have suspected this. You're a clever girl, Jude. You've no doubt started to piece together the clues. I knew the papers were in the house. I knew that despite having business premises, despite having the opportunity to keep those personal documents elsewhere, Michelle would choose to keep them at home. It can't come as a surprise to you to hear that Michelle is not just some internet famous business sensation to me."

That's certainly one way of describing her. Had I stopped to think about the relationship between my blackmailer and my temporary employer, all this could indeed have been obvious to me. I was wrapped up in my own situation. Blackmailed into being here. Fearful for my personal safety. The whys and wherefores of it didn't seem as important as getting the job done.

"The document that I need you to find, the item I really need you to find, is far more valuable to me than the others. Bits and pieces, birth certificate, tax papers, that's all useful down the line, but I need something more."

There's a brief pause, as though the caller is searching for words, and I wait in the heavy silence before they continue.

"What I want could change my life, could change Michelle's life, completely."

My mind is racing. What could possibly cause such disruption? I doubt that Michelle's secret is the same as my own. Even if it were, a simple document couldn't prove that.

"A document?" I ask.

"One document. A single piece of paper. How ironic that paper created Michelle's fortune and a single sheet is going to ruin her."

"But the identity…"

"Forget about those," the voice hisses.

"Why get me to find them?"

"Insurance." The caller delivers the word with a cold finality.

"You said…" I try to recall the words they used. "'*A bartering tool*'?"

"Well, my dear. You stole from Michelle."

"Not yet," I say, remembering my own thoughts and forgetting that I am supposed to be compliant.

The caller laughs. "Is that what you think?" they say. "Well, would you like me to get the police over there and see how they interpret the situation?"

I could go back to her room, replace the documents. Somehow, I don't feel that it would be enough.

"Let's not argue over the details, Jude. I already have enough on you that you're not going to do anything stupid now. The identity papers are also bartering tool against Michelle. When I get what I really need, I can use them…" The caller stops mid-sentence. "Actually, you don't need to know any of this. I've already said too much. Let's stick to the point and get on with the job in hand. You want this to be over, don't you?"

"So much," I say, with an honesty I hadn't planned, and a shrillness that I barely recognise as my own voice.

"Alright." Again, there's a forced hesitance at the other end of the line. Then the caller starts to fill in the outline of the situation.

"Michelle and I had a contract," they say. "We both signed it. We both had a copy. Unfortunately, I trusted her." The voice falters, and I sense how difficult the situation actually might be for them. I can't feel much sympathy for my caller considering what they are holding over me, and what they are making me do, but as the tension comes through, I can't remain completely unmoved. "She destroyed my copy. The only copy that exists is in her possession. I believe it is in that house."

"A contract? What kind of contract?"

"I...she...you don't need to know that."

"I need to know what I'm looking for."

At this moment, this briefest of moments, I feel like the one with the power. It's my turn now to press for information, to take the lead, to have some control. It feels sickeningly good.

"Alright," they say again. "Michelle Crane is not the woman you think she is. She's not the person who the world thinks she is. All this self-made woman bullshit..." The line goes quiet, followed by a muffled sound of movement. There's a click, and I think for a moment that my caller has hung up. My phone display tells me that we are still connected.

My pulse quickens as I wait, my mind working overtime. I'm not sure how I became part of this, why I was chosen, but I'm slowly beginning to understand that the stakes are much higher than I had ever imagined.

"I'm sorry," my caller returns. "I was there at the start," they say. "I was the one with the ideas. Paper Crane was my baby, and Michelle stole that from me. She had the charisma and style; I had the creativity. Apparently, being creative isn't enough to be successful in the twenty-first century. You've got to be a social media darling to get anywhere."

I listen, speechless.

"We had a contract, and I believe she kept it somewhere in that house."

"You believe? You're not sure this time?"

My caller had known without question that the identity papers would be here, but they seem less sure about this contract. If it exists. Can I believe what they are telling me?

What reason would they have to lie?

"I don't think she would risk keeping it anywhere else. If anyone saw it, it would be the end for her. It will be the end for her." There's no gloating in the voice. It's a simple statement of fact.

"Why wouldn't she just destroy it? I mean, if it could cause so much damage to her?"

There's a momentary pause, and the voice comes back with a more resolute, firm tone.

"Jude, dear. I need you to trust me now, and I need you to find that contract."

I already have a gut-wrenching feeling that this task is going to be impossible. I didn't see anything resembling a contract of that kind while I was searching, but I wasn't specifically looking for it. It would be complete madness for Michelle to keep that document in the house. I feel defeated before I even begin.

"And if I don't find it?"

I have to ask the question, even though I don't want to.

"You'll find it. Jude, I believe in you."

And if I don't find it, I'm sure you're going to destroy me too.

TWENTY-SEVEN

In twenty-four hours, Michelle will be home. If I can't locate what I'm looking for in that time, it's not here. If I can't locate it, I'm screwed.

I know I'm going into this search with a negative mindset. I can't understand why Michelle would leave such a potentially damaging document in a home with no security. The only security here is me, and unfortunately for Michelle, I'm not being at all useful.

As I brush through my hair and pull a change of clothes from my travel bag, I try to think of all the places I looked yesterday, and whether there might have been anything remotely like what my caller is asking for.

The whole situation is starting to feel ridiculous.

Still, I'm stuck here. I have to find the contract, but it already seems like a Herculean task. Even if I find it, I suspect my dear blackmailer will come up with some new loophole or technicality. I can't be sure that even if I manage to find this piece of paper in a haystack, I'm going to get the freedom that I was promised.

If I could turn back time and do things differently in my life, I would. But how far would I have to go back to avoid this situation? It seems like I've been constantly hurtling to this point throughout all of my adult life. All the decisions I have made have conspired to bring me here.

"Shit. Shit. Shit." I curse out loud this time. There's nobody around to hear, but I need to let the words escape. I have to release some tension because otherwise I'm going to lose control completely.

I force myself into action.

I get dressed, all the time trying to visualise my route yesterday, bringing to mind everything that I remember seeing. Yes, I shuffled through the invoices in the drawers down in the study, but I didn't check every piece of paper in there.

If I was Michelle, and I wanted to hide an important document, perhaps I would stick it between some other, less significant items. Put the paper in the paper. That could mean a long, drawn-out search for me though.

If I was Michelle, I wouldn't leave that contract here at all. I would have burnt it long ago if I was intent on dishonouring the agreement and having the glory of Paper Crane to myself.

Is Michelle really that type of person? The creamy caramel colours and beaming smiles. The positive taglines on her Insta posts. Girl-boss. Self-made. Heroine for the masses. Is it all one colossal performance?

Even if Paper Crane was someone else's idea, would it have been anything if not for Michelle's charisma and charm? Doesn't she deserve everything she has?

Or does she deserve everything she's going to get?

On with my task: Find the mythical contract, slay the duplicitous influencer.

I'm not sure if this is a fight for justice, or if I'm just being used as part of a wicked plan.

It doesn't matter. I know what I have to do.

Put the gloves back on and get my arse into gear.

As I'm upstairs, it makes sense to check Michelle's room first. That's where I found the identity papers, so there's at least a chance I could have passed over the contract in there. If only I'd known yesterday that I was going to have to find something else, I would have been on the lookout as I searched. Having to go through everything twice is a ridiculous waste of my time.

I suspect that's what my caller wants. It's not just about getting this paper and proving whatever they need to get their share of Paper Crane. They want some power over me, over someone. I would love to sympathise with their situation, but I've been dragged into this in the wrong way for me to give a crap. Could there have been a right way, though?

Even with the doubts I have about what's going to happen even if I find the contract, I don't have any other option.

Or do I?

I stop on the landing, halfway along towards Crane's bedroom as the thought hits me.

What are my other choices?

I could talk to Hester, or even Michelle, and explain why I was looking for the documents, why I took them, and hope that stopping now, before I share them with the blackmailer, would earn me some lenience. I don't have to go any further.

But if I don't, I'm still screwed.

If I back out now, I won't be in any better a situation than I was before I came here. I'm certain that the caller will use what they have against me, and, as they have rightly assumed, doing that will destroy my life.

How absolutely perfect it must have seemed to my caller when they found me. So well placed to do what they wanted. So easy to manipulate.

It all seems a little too perfect.

The more I think about it, the more certain I am that there's a deeper scheme at work here.

For now, though, I have to keep looking. The clock is ticking, and I have a bad feeling that I am going to be spending every minute searching in vain.

Although I didn't plan to stop here, as I think through my limited options, I realise I'm standing outside the door to the next guest suite. I haven't stepped foot inside any of the other bedrooms, and I feel drawn to look inside now. I push open the door.

The suite is surprisingly bare and bland compared to my own guest room. The walls are painted in a blank magnolia, and the bed, nowhere near as grand as the one I have been sleeping in, is dressed in plain white. Although this room is roughly the same size as mine, it looks much bigger, because apart from the bed, the space is devoid of any other furniture. I had imagined that each of the guest rooms would be elaborately styled in the same way as mine. Michelle is a socialite, after all; being social is her *thing*. Wouldn't she want to be prepared for unannounced drop-ins or spontaneous overnight stays?

I step into the room and the thuds of my footsteps echo as I walk across to the window. There's no carpet, only ivory-painted boards. This room is minimal to the point of bleak.

Then it hits me.

This could be Hester's room.

If it were to be her room, the difference between this and the rest of the house would make sense. She would surely have been able to choose her own style, have her room decorated as she wished. She and Michelle appear close, I'm sure Hester's employer would want her to feel at home here.

And yet it feels the opposite of homely.

It couldn't be any more cold and unwelcoming. But then again, neither could Hester.

I bob my head down to look beneath the bed.

There's just empty space.

No wardrobe, no drawers, no storage. I have to look more closely at the walls to make sure I'm not missing any hidden panels or secret sliding compartments that will make a whole other room appear. There's nothing. No walk-in closet. No sign of anything belonging to Hester at all.

In the en suite there's exactly the same fixtures and products as there is in mine. It's almost like a hotel. A very dismal, bleak hotel.

If this is Hester's room, she is really making a statement with it. I'm not sure that I have worked out what that is yet.

I'm probably a philistine. This décor is no doubt the latest trend, and if I was with the whole living my life on social media thing, perhaps I would understand it. It's not like the walls are painted in virgin's blood. It's plain, functional, and really it looks fine. I wouldn't have even thought twice about it unless I'd seen how well co-ordinated the rest of the house is.

Down to the crockery.

I shake my head and leave the room.

At least it's one less place to search.

Back on the landing, I give in to curiosity as I reach the next guest room. The weight of time passing is growing heavy, even with almost a full day ahead of me. Still, I push the door open and look inside.

It's another white shell of a room.

It shouldn't feel strange.

But it does.

My nerves are shot. I have every right to be suspicious, paranoid, messed up in the head.

This whole setup is just plain crazy.

I go into the room and survey it, and then do the same again for the third guest room, which is also pale, heartless, and empty.

Maybe it's easier to dress up these blank canvases if Michelle wants to use them for photoshoots. Maybe it's just a cool girl thing that I don't have a clue about. Maybe I just don't have time to overthink anymore.

I find no answers.
I find nothing.
I move on.

When I reach Michelle's bedroom, the afternoon sun is streaming through the windows, reflecting off the warm honey walls. The atmosphere is completely different from yesterday evening when I was shining my torch around the room. In the daytime, the light in here is perfect.

I have to reach out a hand and steady myself against the drawer unit as the realisation hits me.

When I came in here last night, the drapes were half-closed; now the curtains are tied back.

Hester must have been up here.

She's the only other person who's been inside the house.

I think back, quickly. I was asleep on the sofa when Hester came in. Wasn't I? I heard the front entrance open, Hester walking through the atrium. But what if that's not what I heard? What if she was already in the house? She could have been here for hours, and I wouldn't have known. I was exhausted; I'd probably have slept even longer if she hadn't come into the living room.

Hester could have been anywhere.

She could have been in my bedroom.

She could have searched my bag.

She could know what I have done.

What if she's biding her time, just waiting for Michelle to come home so that she can be all goody goody, the heroine saving the day, telling Crane what I've done?

No, no, no.

My legs are jellified, but I force myself to straighten up, and walk as quickly as I can back down the landing to my room. I have to know that the papers are still there. I have to see them bundled in my bag. She can't have found them. She can't have taken them.

No, no, no.

I thrust my hand into my bag and rearrange the layers, waiting for my gloved fingers to make contact with the paper.

They do.

The documents are still there.

I let out a breath that I'd been purposefully holding. I couldn't let myself relax until I knew the papers were still in my possession.

Hester knows nothing.

She might have been in the house earlier than I thought, but I've covered my tracks well. There's no sign of disturbance. No sign that I've done anything wrong here.

A jubilant cry rises from deep within me, and I let it ring around my room.

It's too early to celebrate anything yet, but my relief is too great to keep bundled inside me. I'm still in the game, and it intensifies with every passing minute.

TWENTY-EIGHT

Libby

I knew when I left Neil and my former life that going back into project management was a no-no. Still, for some reason I imagined that someone with a skill set like mine would be able to step into a new job without much trouble. Let's just say that I seriously underestimated the situation.

Three weeks after moving into the flat, I'm beginning to see that the employment market isn't exactly the smorgasbord of opportunity that I thought it was. Realistically, I need to find something, anything, before the end of next month. I calculated living expenses for three months in my escape plan, and by the end of that period, I need to have my new life up and running.

Being overcautious is holding me back. Even though I know that there's a decent amount of physical distance between Neil and me now, I can't shake the thought that at any given time he could track me down, drag me back, punish me…

I don't want to think about it.

I can't call on my past work references to vouch for me. If Neil called them, asked if I had been in touch, if they knew where I was, I'm not sure that anyone would be sensible or sensitive enough to keep my new location a secret. The problem with the kind of abuse that he exercised was that I kept it all to myself. It was mostly invisible to the outside world. My employers never knew what was going on at home, and my co-workers clearly didn't, or perhaps they might have been more understanding and less callous towards me. But then maybe I would never have left.

I have my life back now, but at what cost?

I shudder at the thought. Things are tough now; the prospect of not finding work terrifies me, but not as much as the idea of being with Neil.

Every now and then I let myself wonder what he's doing, whether he tried to look for me after I left, and, if so, how soon he gave up. A part of me thinks he didn't even know that what he was doing was wrong. But I try to silence that part of me. If he didn't know, then it wasn't his fault. I can't accept that. It's not as though everyone who loses their job ends up beating their partner and controlling every aspect of their lives. There's no point in hashing over the details. I don't want to think about the pain I've left behind. My past is my past now. I don't think Neil will ever come looking for me, and I hope he doesn't even want to.

For now, though, I've got to think about the present, and how I'm going to get by if I don't find a job very soon.

I know the situation is becoming dire, but still, I force myself to check exactly what kind of shit I'm in. I click open the app on my phone, silently praying that some miracle has occurred, and some random unknown benefactor has made an immense deposit into my account. I'm still in credit, but the grand total of all my worldly funds is £162.

Three months seemed like plenty of time to get myself set up in my new life, but despite the best of my efforts – and I've tried every day – I have got nowhere.

£162 won't even cover my food costs for another month, let alone bills and rent.

I came from a life where, on paper, I had enough money for an expensive car, designer clothes, pointless pricey accessories and a costly workbag filled with high-end products. Now I can't justify a bus trip unless it's essential for my job search. I have the single bag of clothes I brought with me, and the most valuable item I own is my laptop. I can't possibly part with that; it's my link to the outside world of employment. I don't have any way of making money other than getting out there again today and hoping that someone, anyone, will give me a chance.

Neil lost his job, and I carried him for three years. I have nobody to support me. All I have is myself.

It's still better than being with him.

I try to scrape together a positive mental attitude from the dregs of motivation I have left. Being rejected day after day must be hard for anyone, but when you're used to being headhunted from one post to another, it's soul destroying.

My usual get-out-there-and-find-a-job outfit comprises a plain navy dress and flat shoes. Not exactly dressed-up, but not quite casual. Whatever I come across on my journey today, this should work. I brush my hair and tie it back in a simple ponytail. No more annoying Neil with the hairdryer in the mornings, but no more prestigious products either. Since I've (partially involuntarily) ditched the designer brand toiletries and switched to Aldi's own, I've not noticed any diffcrence. I wonder how much money I was wasting when I was with Neil. Whatever it was, spending on what he thought were essentials was the only way I could access any of my income. Now, those essentials don't seem quite as essential after all.

After trying for ten weeks to find administrative or office jobs online, now I'm down to my last couple of hundred pounds, I know I need a stopgap. I'm not giving up on finding something more – how can I put this? – *me*, but I need to make some money and I need to do it fast.

I shouldn't have relied so heavily on finding the kind of work that I want to do, but when I signed up at the local admin temping agencies, they made it sound as though I'd be turning down jobs within the week.

I've not had any offers from any of the three companies I signed up with.

Not enough experience.

A blank CV.

And my references? Because I couldn't exactly call upon the companies I worked with before, I've had to use some poetic license there. A few dummy emails for people that don't actually exist. My life is a fabrication; my history is fictitious now. I have a false name and a desperate need to avoid any links with my past life. I still think of myself as Libby Halstead, but I left that name behind me when I left Neil. I'm easing into a new identity, but the new me doesn't have an employment history. And that sucks.

So now it's down to the wire and out to the town centre.

I'm sure that when I was comfortably employed, sliding seamlessly from one company to the next, I used to see signs in windows all the time saying, '*staff wanted*', '*temp jobs available*' and the like. Maybe the area I moved to is already well served with shop workers and baristas, or maybe I didn't see as many of those signs as I think I did.

I walk almost the length of the high street before I finally see a note in the window of a café. It's a greasy little place, the kind of eatery that I would never visit as a customer. I pause for a moment to reconsider that thought. I don't have the funds that I used to. My budget doesn't cover lunches every day from Pret anymore. Looking at the menu that hangs above the note it looks as though my funds wouldn't even stretch to this place. I swallow my snobbery and read the sign again.

"Waitress wanted. Immediate start. Come and talk to us."

No mention of the wages, and the gender-specific '*waitress*' gives me a bad vibe, but I need a job. Any job. 'Immediate start' sounds perfect, so I focus on that, take a deep breath, and open the door.

TWENTY-NINE

Jude

I can't find the contract.

It's as simple and as complicated as that.

I can't find it.

THIRTY

Shit.

THIRTY-ONE

Libby

The old-fashioned bell that rings when I push open the door and walk into the café matches the old-fashioned gender-specific tone of the note. I don't have the luxury of caring about that, so I check my posture, hold my head high, and walk purposefully to the counter.

"Take a seat, love. Someone will be over with a menu."

The voice comes through from another room, out of sight, to the rear of the front-facing customer service area.

I don't feel comfortable shouting through; it feels unprofessional. Still, this is a different world from the one that I'm used to inhabiting, so I bite the bullet and reply.

"I'm here about the job," I call, trying to keep my voice sounding light and friendly.

"Oh!"

The surprise in the response is obvious. It feels like they haven't heard this before, which seems like both a good thing and a bad thing. I would have thought that with so few opportunities available in town there would be a line of potential employees. Still, it also means that I'm in with a chance. This is temporary; I'm willing to do just about anything now.

A woman's head pops around the door between the back room and main café area. At first glance, she looks to be in her fifties, with a blue hairnet messily sitting on top of fluffy blonde curls and a white plastic apron over her dusty-looking black top. When she steps out and comes closer, I realise my estimation was way off. We must be around the same age: early thirties.

She eyes me, sizing me up before speaking.

"You local?" she asks.

"I live locally," I reply. I know that my accent doesn't match hers. I don't fit in around here yet. I'm not sure that's a decent way to assess my suitability for the job though.

"But you're not from round here, are you?"

I try not to frown. I do my best to keep that positive mental attitude as I reply, "Not originally, no."

She doesn't need to know how long I've been here. I'm definitely not going to get into where I came from or why. This is a simple waitressing job in a run-down café, not a CEO position in a multi-million-pound company.

"Have you done this kind of work before?"

"Yes," I lie. "I used to work in a little café like this back home."

I try to make it sound as though this is my true vocation, that all I have ever dreamed of is pouring coffee and wiping down tables.

"Like this?" the woman says, picking up on my word choice. "And tell me, love. What do you think this café is like?"

I think on my feet, because even if waitressing is not my forte, responding well under pressure is.

I look around for show, and to give myself a few moments longer for those thoughts to form. There are six Formica-topped tables, each with four mis-matched plastic chairs around them. The walls are a bland grey, and there's a noticeable smear of ketchup splashed next to one of the tables. Dried on, not fresh. The floor is sticky linoleum, and the last time it was cleaned was probably when I was still working, hell it could have even been when Neil was still working. I'm struggling to find something positive to say. If I had any other option, I wouldn't be so desperate to please this brusque, sour woman, and I certainly wouldn't be trying to talk her into letting me have a job here.

But I am desperate.

And I don't have any other options.

"Places like this have personality," I say. "Not like those chains and franchises that are taking over everywhere now. I'm sure your customers come here for you, just as much as they do for the food you sell. It's about…"

It's on the tip of my tongue to say that she is selling a feeling and give her some blurb about branding and customer influencing, but I'm supposed to be a waitress, not a strategist.

"It's about people. A person. You." My misstep causes me to stumble over the words, and I know I haven't delivered my best sales pitch.

"How absolutely lovely of you to say," she says, her words flat and unconvincing. "I'm sure you think that coming in here and piling on the compliments is going to get you a job…"

My heart sinks. I can already tell what's coming next.

"But if I wanted false flattery, I'd get on Tinder, not stick a note up in the window looking for a waitress."

"Right," I say, trying to summon up any words that might change her mind. I've worked in project management for years, and I've dealt with some tough cookies along the way, but this woman actually takes the biscuit.

The cake display on the counter is obviously influencing my thoughts. They don't look fresh, and, apart from one gateau that's had a slice cut from it, they appear untouched.

"Look, perhaps you could give me a chance for a few days and…"

"Appreciate you stopping by," she says with a firm, unfriendly smile.

I can already tell that it would be pointless to try to sway her. She made up her mind as soon as she heard me speak. Perhaps she even decided as soon as she saw me. Who knows what causes a person to judge someone else? I made my assumptions about her, and she made hers about me.

This is another job to add to the list of missed opportunities.

I smile, nod politely and thank the woman. We never even got to exchange names.

If the cakes had been even slightly appealing, I might have bought a slice to take with me. Nothing takes the taste out of black forest gateau like disappointment and the threat of impending destitution.

Instead, when I walk back down the high street, I step into Pret and buy a latte and a chocolate brownie. I know it's a luxury that I can't afford, but it feels like sticking two fingers up at prissy Miss Café. Besides, I need the sugar rush to pick me up, because I have no idea what I'm going to do now.

THIRTY-TWO

Jude

I have no idea what I'm going to do now.

The light of the afternoon has melted into the shadows of late evening, and I've searched the entire house. Six hours; every drawer, cupboard, unit I can find. I've taken the books down from the bookshelves and shaken them; that's how desperate things have become.

Nothing.

The two storerooms that Michelle swept me past on our tour of the house – was it only a few days ago? – were useless. Rails of clothing, hats on wooden posts mounted on the walls, jewellery. Perhaps those are the kind of things a regular thief would target. There must be thousands of pounds' worth of outfits and accessories stored away, so easy to slip into my bag and take with me. Michelle probably wouldn't even notice anything was missing.

I'm not interested in them though, no matter how simple it would be.

I just need to find that contract.

But I don't think it's even here.

I've exhausted every conceivable hiding spot in this house.

Nothing.

My phone has remained silent throughout my search. The caller obviously knows that I'm going to be kept busy with the task they've assigned me. But I can't complete it. I've looked everywhere. Literally everywhere. There are no more false bottoms to any drawers. No secret passages, no sliding walls behind bookcases.

I flop down onto the sofa in defeated desperation.

Should I unpick the seams of the sofa cushions? Look inside there? Start digging up the garden in case there's a hidden treasure chest buried that holds the single stupid piece of paper I need?

"It's not here!"

I shout the words into the empty room.

I know my caller can't hear me, not here, not while I'm alone in this luxury prison that I'm trapped inside.

Everything in this house is designed to be comfortable, calming, and clean, but I feel the opposite of each of those.

I have hated myself in the past. When I made difficult decisions, the decisions that got me here, I hated myself. But this? This is something else.

I hate myself.

I hate this situation.

I hate this feeling of absolute loss of control.

Resting my head in my hands, I can't hold back the tears any longer. I sit on Michelle Crane's opulent brown sofa and sob. Tears stream down my hot cheeks, flowing for the hopelessness of the predicament that I am in, and for the potential consequences I face if I don't fulfil my caller's demand.

There's one inescapable fact: I can't find that contract.

I would never have stopped the search if I thought there was anywhere else that I could look, but I have to accept the truth: I am defeated.

Crying won't help, but I can't stop the body-shuddering pain escaping me.

Let it out, I tell myself. *Let it out and then get it the hell together.*

I give myself a couple of minutes of weakness before sitting up straight, taking a few deep, long breaths, and trying to get my head together.

I've been through this before, thinking about the worst-case scenario.

What would happen if the caller does reveal my secrets?

I need to think about it more logically. Until now, I thought all I had to do was carry out the caller's requests and I could save myself. Now I know that it's impossible, I have to create a *Plan B*. I should have done this from the start; I realise that now. I was so caught up in the threat of losing everything I've worked for that I didn't stop to think that there could be another way.

What would happen if the caller does reveal my secrets?

I'd have to move on, start again. I couldn't work as a house sitter with people knowing about my past. For the purposes of my brainstorming, I'm discounting the chance that the caller will reveal that I've stolen documents from Michelle. How would they know if they weren't in on it? An anonymous tip-off could land me deep in the shit, though.

There's one solution to this. If they are going to reveal what I've done anyway, I could put the papers back. Right now. I don't need to steal them if the caller is going to spill my secrets, anyway. If they do that, they have nothing else to threaten me with. If I can accept the inevitable, no matter how hard that is, I can regain some power.

This thought makes me smile, even in the fraught situation I'm in.

The caller has slipped up by giving me an impossible task. If I lose everything by not carrying out all of their requests, but there's no chance of me finding that contract, then I'm going to lose everything, anyway. There's absolutely no benefit to me giving them the papers. They are going to have to find some other sucker and blackmail them.

Unless I tell Michelle.

The thought comes to me in a flash of brilliance.

If the caller is going to reveal my secrets anyway, I don't have to leave Michelle Crane open to a future attack. She obviously knows my caller. They worked together. They had this dumb contract. That gives me an option: I can tell her everything, reveal the entire plot. It doesn't help me, but at least I might be able to feel better about myself and less like a piece of dirt for ever coming here like this in the first place.

My tears have dried now. Instead, I have a surge of energy and excitement. I'm not powerless after all. I have choices. I don't have to make bad decisions this time.

My caller is going to do what they threatened to do, regardless.

I have to live with that. I'm going to need to plan for my future, but I can do it.

A tiny voice tells me I could take Michelle's papers for myself. I could use them. It's a ridiculous thought. Much as stealing from the storerooms is unthinkable for me, taking those documents for my own personal financial gain is also completely off the table. There's no way that I would ever do anything like that.

But look at what I was prepared to do.

I was going to destroy Michelle's life.

And for what? To save my own?

What makes me any more worthy than her?

Is she a bad person because she dishonoured some agreement with someone she used to work with? I don't know the facts. I only have my caller's side of the story, and I don't even know much of that. They're hardly on my list of most trustworthy sources, anyway.

I've done my share of awful things. I don't think I'm in a position to judge anyone else. If it's up to the person without sin to cast the first stone, I won't be throwing anything.

Just as I think that the fog in my thoughts is lifting, the phone rings.

THIRTY-THREE

Sitting in Michelle's lavish living room, a bead of perspiration trickles down my forehead. My heart thuds like a war drum as I hear the ominous ringing from my phone. I haven't had time to decide. I don't know which way I'm going to play this.

Before despair can tighten its grip, I reach my trembling hand into my pocket and draw out the phone.

"Hello?" I answer, my voice unable to conceal my anxiety. I suspect the caller already knows exactly what kind of tension I'm feeling.

"You disappoint me, Jude," the voice sneers, sending icy tendrils down my spine. "Have you given up already?"

Instinctively, I look around. I know my caller can't see me. There's no way for them to know that I haven't found what I'm looking for. Still, I look. But of course, if I had already found the contract, I would have phoned them before now.

I'm not thinking rationally. My thoughts are skipping to conclusions, and I'm not focusing on things that could turn out to be important later.

"No," I say, defensively. I rethink and change my answer. "Yes. I can't find it anywhere. I've searched the entire house. There's no sign of the contract. I give up."

Although I'm trying my best to keep my voice calm and steady, I can hear the shakiness beneath my words, betraying my emotions.

A chilling chuckle emanates from the other end of the line. "Oh, but you're missing something, dear Jude. Look closer, pay attention to the details. You'll find what you seek."

The more I hear, the more convinced I am that this is all part of some game. But who is in control of it, and why?

They seem to know where the contract is. Their statement sounds like a riddle. I'm through with this.

"What do you want from me?" I demand, my voice shaking with a mix of fear and defiance. "Who are you, and why are you doing this?"

"You know what I want." The caller's voice is clear and cold. "You don't need to know who I am, and I'm sure you can work out why I am doing this."

"Why me though? Why choose me? What have I ever done to deserve this?" I never planned to say any of these words, nevertheless they are spilling from my mouth. "I made a mistake, okay? I know that. I would never have done what I did unless I had to."

"And you wouldn't have done *this* unless you had to either, would you? That's exactly why you're the ideal person for the job. When the chips are down, you do what you need to do, regardless of whether it's wrong or right. Regardless of the potential consequences."

There's a strange mix of admiration and bitterness in the caller's voice. Whatever they think about me, they're right.

"I don't have to do this," I say, again without thinking it through. I wish I'd had more time before the caller phoned me. I wish I could have decided on my action plan. All I have are half-shaped ideas.

"Oh, but you do, my dear…"

I cut off the sentence. "…or you'll destroy me. Yes. You've told me what the price of my failure will be."

I hardly recognise the person who's talking now. This isn't like me, or at least it isn't like the person I've been for the past few years as a house sitter. My life has been shattered before, and I have picked up the shards and rebuilt a new life. I've reinvented myself more than once, and I know that if it comes down to it, I can do it again.

The line is silent. Not quite silent. I can hear the caller's heavy breaths. I know they are still there.

I fill the empty space. "If you know where the contract is, tell me and let's be done with this. I don't have the energy to keep playing your game. I'm stressed and tired and sick of this bullshit."

I guess when my back's to the wall and I realise I haven't really got any options, this is who I become.

"And if you aren't going to tell me," I continue, "you'd better start that whole *'destroying my life'* thing now. If I can't find the contract, I can't win. You've rigged this…" I struggle to spit out the final word, "…game."

"Game. Game. Game. You keep using that word, Jude, but you have no real idea what's going on here."

"Then tell me!" I yell the words into the room. This is it. I've actually cracked.

The voice at the other end of the line responds to my outburst by speaking more quietly, in a calm, measured tone. "Okay, Jude. Everything will become clear. Your secrets are safe. Don't do anything foolish." They actually sigh before continuing. "The contract is there. Okay? I know that it's there because I hid it there."

"What?" I'm incensed by the revelation after all the time I have spent searching. My face is burning, and I can feel tears resurfacing, this time through anger rather than sadness.

"I left the contract there. Find it."

With that, the line goes dead, leaving me with more questions than answers. I struggle to regain my composure. *My secret is safe*, they said. What does that even mean? That I don't have to find the contract to get out of here unscathed? That I still need to deliver the documents? I have even less of a clue what's going on than before we spoke to each other again.

Now, I am filled with determination to uncover whatever hidden truth has brought me to this point. I refuse to let the blackmailer's mind games break me. The emotional swings of the past hour are overwhelming, and I'm utterly exhausted. I don't know how much longer I can carry this on.

Taking a deep breath, I start to retrace my steps through the opulent living area, my eyes scanning every inch of the carefully curated space. My hands trace the edges of picture frames, the corners of furniture, searching for any hidden compartments or clues.

The contract is here, somewhere.

Look closer, pay attention to the details.

I don't want to play this game, but even though my caller has said that there aren't going to be any repercussions, for some twisted, sick reason I want to keep searching. I won't be defeated.

THIRTY-FOUR

Libby

Back in my crappy flat, I open my laptop once again.

Please, please, this time. Please let there be something for me, someone who will give me a chance.

My anti-virus subscription has ended, and I can't afford to renew. The pop-ups offer me penis extensions, unbeatable wins on this week's bingo games and hot women in my area that are apparently desperate to meet me.

I doubt it, ladies. I doubt it very much.

I click the windows closed and wonder how far up Maslow's hierarchy of needs spam free web browsing comes.

I have a routine, when it comes to checking the job sites, but I don't have time to wait for any of the decent jobs. There's not enough give in my bank account to let me apply for an admin role, wait for the deadline to pass and for the HR staff at the other end of the paper chain to select their candidates. After that, I would need to be interviewed, pass the selection procedure, and wait out the recruitment limbo period between being chosen and actually starting work.

Despite the sticky sweet aftertaste of the chocolate brownie in my mouth, the whole business with the woman in the café has jarred my confidence to a new low. If I can't even get a job in a greasy spoon, how can I expect to find work in an office? I have no credentials that I can speak of. My years of experience and specialist skills are no good to me when using them would only create a paper trail back to Neil.

Even if he's not looking for me, I have no doubt that if he found information leading to my whereabouts, my life would be over. There wouldn't be another chance of escape, that's for sure.

I should have killed him when I had the chance.

I laugh at the random thought that entered my head, and then frown at the fact that it popped up at all. I've never done a single bad thing in my life. Of course, everyone says that and forgets about the fifty pence they borrowed out of their mum's pocket when they were a kid, or the library book that they neglected to return and is still on their bookshelf twelve years later. I don't have any of my books anymore. I don't have my mum anymore. If I've ever done anything bad, it was nothing anywhere near as serious as planning to murder my ex-husband.

Husband.

Despite the miles between us, I have to remind myself that on paper, he is still my husband.

Two whole years he would need to wait to divorce me for abandonment. Me? I don't care either way. I'm never going to marry again, so what difference does it make? I no longer have his name. As long as I can stay as far away from Neil as possible, I don't care about the marriage contract.

Thinking about him does nothing to help me in my current predicament. Unless I decide to pop back home and ask him for a loan, of course.

I would let myself laugh, but the desperation of my situation holds me back.

There's nothing new on the job sites. No updates from the agencies. I call each of them anyway, just to hear from an actual real-life human that no, they haven't found a suitable placement for someone of my skill profile yet.

Skill profile.

I'd put a bet on the fact that one of those agencies is using a system that I helped to implement with my *skill profile*.

I keep my irritation under control and respond politely to the agency assistants. When I hang up the phone, I can't stop myself bursting into tears.

Maybe I can drag this out for another few weeks past the end of the month. A late rent payment is more acceptable than a missed one. I'll get reminders for the bills before my services are cut off. If I can make the money stretch for food while I just eek it out and find something, anything, I can buy more time. I should never have splurged on the coffee and cake, and the sweet taste in my mouth is making me feel sick.

No admin jobs, no service jobs.

I'm screwed.

I look back at my laptop, ready to log out of my agency accounts, close down the search for another day, and another pop-up window appears.

Girls, girls, girls!

It's a large box, this time, taking up almost half of the screen. In centre view is a woman sitting on a bed, a pastel floral duvet cover beneath her, just the kind of thing I'd pick out if I was able to shop anymore. Something about how normal it looks makes me smile.

Don't watch porn! Chat now to girls who are waiting for YOU.

"I'm not planning on doing either," I say to the screen, and slowly reach out to shut down the computer.

And then I stop.

I stop, and that is when my world changes again, for the second pivotal time.

I pull back and look at the woman on the screen. She's in her underwear. Not naked. Her room looks like any regular bedroom in any street, any town. There's nothing special about her. There are no props;

it's just her, wiggling and wriggling for the camera.

I flick my eyes up to the top of my laptop screen and remember all the online meetings I had when face-to-face conferences were impossible. My laptop has a webcam. I have a suitably dull bedroom.

I could…

I shake my head.

I could…

Really, this isn't me.

I have £150 to my name. Is dancing in my underwear really such a bad thought? It's not like I'd be in some grimy club where men could reach out and touch me or ask for more than I'm willing to give. I'd be in control.

I've forgotten what that feels like.

But I could. Perhaps I could.

THIRTY-FIVE

Jude

Just as I had decided to give up the search, the call from the blackmailer has given me fresh determination to not be beaten. There must be something I've missed; the caller said so. Pay attention to the details. This is so messed up, but now that it's becoming clearer that something more complicated is at play here, I'm too intrigued to stop.

If I find the contract, that doesn't mean I have to give it to the caller. I'm not obligated to do anything. I can decide later what I'm going to do. If I find it. When I find it.

You wouldn't have done this unless you had to.

I can almost hear the echo of the caller's words as I walk around the living area.

I know it's there because I hid it there.

It makes no sense. The only way it could make any sense is if Michelle destroyed her own copy and the caller, my blackmailer, her former business partner, thought that hiding their own copy here was the only way to keep it safe. Is Michelle the sort of person who would track someone down and search *their* property for a copy of the document that could lead to her downfall? Who knows what lengths someone would go to in order to save themselves? I'm only just learning what I would do, let alone make guesses about anyone else's limitations.

If Michelle has really built this business on lies, the truth could ruin her reputation. For a woman who has made her fortune through her online persona and charismatic presence, a secret of this magnitude would surely cause more damage than any kind of identity theft.

Destroying her reputation would ruin her life.

Destroying my reputation would ruin mine.

There's one other question that I can't shake off. Why now? Why has the blackmailer suddenly decided to get me involved now? What's the urgency to expose Michelle after all this time? Paper Crane has been a successful business for years now. If my caller has been screwed over by Michelle, why would they wait so long to reveal her secrets?

My mind spins as I pick up photographs, checking for hidden paper behind the smiling images. *Look closer.* I shake my head.

I've searched this house twice over. I'm sure I've looked closely in every room, at every piece of paper in this picture-perfect home.

Paper.

It hits me like a lightning bolt.

A grin bursts across my face.

Of course. I should have guessed.

I should have picked up on the clues.

I know for certain that my caller has hidden the contract in plain sight, somewhere that Michelle would see it every day and not even notice it was there.

I know where the contract is. I just don't know what I'm going to do with that information. Not yet.

THIRTY-SIX

Libby

Setting up the account is easy, at least technically. Apparently, the webcam service provider, as I've chosen to refer to my new employer, is more than happy to welcome new girls, girls, girls, with open arms. They don't ask for references or employment history. My made-up CV is useless now. All they want is a willingness for me to perform.

The psychological aspect is more difficult. Once I start down this path, there's no going back. This will always be a part of who I am, of what I am.

I have to be certain before I do this.

As much as I have told myself that this is a short-term, temporary solution, I know the ramifications are going to be long-lasting. How could they not be? If I ever meet a man in the future that I want to have a relationship with, and I'm not sure at all that I ever will, I'm going to have to tell him about this. If I didn't tell him, and somehow he found out it would be far worse.

I will find another job. This isn't forever.

A part of me wonders how many women before me have thought the same thing.

I make up a screen name, another new identity, and somehow that helps me to distance myself from the person I'm about to become and the things I'll have to do. Setting up my payment details is more satisfying. I'll make around £2 per minute when I'm on screen. That's £120 every hour, although what I'll find to do for a full sixty minutes is beyond me. I could earn more by providing additional services, but that's a step too far. Stripping to my underwear is my limit, and even that makes my skin crawl. Having strangers paying money to watch me dance around in my bedroom is a bizarre thought. I can't let myself go further than that and consider what they might be doing while they watch me.

I'm not the most attractive woman, but I'm certainly not ugly. I've had three years of being mostly ignored sexually by my husband, but that still doesn't mean that I want dodgy old men slapping their meat to my image. The taste of bile in my throat stops my thoughts in their tracks.

They won't be dodgy old men, I tell myself. *Maybe they just want to chat with a woman.*

I don't get paid any extra for conversation, but I checked the box when I signed up to say that I offered it as a service. Getting paid for just talking to someone seems like a breeze. Getting paid at all seems like a miracle at this point.

As long as I stay in control of what I do, and make choices that suit me, I can do this.

This is my way out of a shitty situation.

It's not forever.

THIRTY-SEVEN

Jude

When I have the contract in my grasp I finally feel as though I can relax. I have a few options now, but I don't know what I'm going to do.

I could hand everything over to my blackmailer. Whether they're going to reveal my secrets or not is a mystery to me. I have so many unanswered questions that it's hard for me to work out what the truth is.

I could hand everything over to Michelle. I'm fairly sure that she didn't know the contract was in her house. It was well hidden,

251

but it wasn't hidden at all. I just needed to look more closely, as my caller said. Handing over the contract also entails telling Michelle the truth about everything, and whatever consequences that might bring for me.

I could put the documents and the contract back where I found them, leave with nothing, and see what happens next. I don't need to be involved in this shitshow situation. I've been dragged into it because my caller thinks I'm some kind of useful tool, or just a pawn for them to play with. I don't have to be under their control. I can take control for myself. And if they reveal my secrets? I will have to rebuild my life again.

A part of me thinks that I should have thought about that in the first place. If I had told my blackmailer that they could do whatever they wanted with my secrets and I didn't care, I would never have ended up here. At the time though, keeping my past under wraps seemed like the most important thing in the world. Losing the life I have built would be devastating — but I would recover. If nothing else good has come out of this weekend, I've learnt an important lesson.

What happens when you lose everything? You just start again.

With that in mind, I treat myself to the soak in the bath that I considered yesterday. As the deep tub fills with hot water, I pour a generous dose of the Diptyque foam and swirl it until the bubbles blossom.

I step out of my clothes and slide into the water. Even a long bathe won't be able to relieve the weight of this weekend. I let the suds caress me and breath in the aroma. The scent is a dark floral dream, and for a split second I wish that this was all mine: the house, the persona, the lifestyle, the fame. What would it be like to be Michelle Crane?

If there's one thing I've learnt, it's that being popular and famous isn't an easy ride. Success invites sabotage. When you're at the top of your field, like Michelle is, there are always people that want to bring you down, and as they say, the higher you climb, the harder you fall. My tumble from grace would be enough to destroy the life I have, but I could get back on my feet again. Michelle wouldn't be able to up and move to a different town, start over, and fade away into the background. She's far too recognisable to escape from her past.

I lie in the tub until the water cools and the skin on my fingers becomes a prune like pucker. When I pull myself out, I feel lighter, less burdened, as though some of my troubles have been washed away. What I have really lost is the fear of being exposed. Whatever happens happens. I can deal with it. I can move on. I am going to be fine.

So convinced and confident am I that after getting out of the bath I switch off my phone – something I haven't dared do since the calls from my blackmailer began. I have been under their control every second of the day. Now, no matter what happens, I'm in control of my own destiny.

I need to think. I need to make my own decisions now.

Whatever decision I make is going to have long-lasting effects, for Michelle, and for me. Whatever I choose is going to affect someone's life. I came here to save myself, but now, well, I'm not sure what I'm going to do.

THIRTY-EIGHT

By the time 3pm, Monday afternoon comes around I've had plenty of thinking time.

My bag is packed and waiting by the front door, and I'm in the living room, finally relaxing on the sofa before Michelle arrives home. My mind is so focused on waiting for the homeowner to return that I hear the sound of the gates as soon as they open. The sound of tyres on gravel is unmistakable. It's time.

It's Michelle.

She's home.

From where I'm sitting, I can see Hester holding the door open as Michelle breezes through. She's got her handbag looped over her arm but must have left her luggage for Hester to deal with.

"Jude!" she says, as if greeting a friend rather than someone she's employed to look after her house for the weekend.

She walks into the living room and leans in towards me for a hug.

I awkwardly half-stand to meet her embrace and smile.

"Hi," I say. "Good trip?"

"Oh, you know," she says, gesticulating with her arm, as if that tells me all I need to know.

I nod in return.

"The trip was fine," she clarifies, "but planes, ugh. I'm never going to enjoy flying."

The last time I flew anywhere was when I was a kid, and I'd love the chance to go somewhere – anywhere – now. Maybe I will. I could leave the country, start again somewhere new and far away.

"How was the house? Did you have a good weekend? Anything exciting to report? Cat burglars? Marauding fans?"

She beams a smile to show that she's joking and then sits next to me.

I can hear Hester in the atrium bringing through the luggage. I'd like to get away before I get embroiled in any further conversation.

"Yes, thanks so much," I say. "It was fine. Incident free. I'm sorry, but I really can't stay any longer."

"Are you sure?" Michelle asks with greater enthusiasm than I would expect from someone who's been travelling for the past few hours. "We've hardly had time to chat."

I get to see that social media famous smile again, and I remember for a moment that countless followers would give anything to be here, in this house, with this woman. I, on the other hand, would give anything to be walking out of the door.

Even though I've never been a fan of Michelle's, per se, in other circumstances I would probably have stayed, just for the hell of it. It's not every day you get to have a conversation with such a well-known figure.

"Really. I'm sorry," I say.

Hester strides purposefully into the room and settles on the other sofa. She says nothing but watches me as I stand and reach out to shake Michelle's hand.

"Okay," Michelle says, sounding a little hurt. "Well, thanks for everything. I'll be sure to leave you some positive feedback."

"Thanks," I reply. "It's been a pleasure."

It's been an absolute rollercoaster, and I'm thankful to be leaving, but I choose to make the polite response instead.

"Let me show you out," Hester says.

"I can…" I start to turn down her offer, but she cuts me off with a wave of her hand.

"No problem," she says, walking beside me to the exit.

When we reach the door, she looks over her shoulder towards Michelle. Crane isn't paying any attention to us; she's already taken out her phone and is caught up in her scrolling.

I feel as though Hester is about to say something to me, but she opens the door and stands aside. An eerie shudder passes through me as I walk past Hester, out of Michelle Crane's house, and into the sunshine.

My car has been sitting patiently, parked at the front of the house, since Saturday afternoon. So much has happened since I last sat behind the wheel that I almost feel like a different person as I slide back into the driver's seat. I throw my bag onto the passenger seat and slip my key into the ignition.

Without looking back, I shift into first and head towards the exit. I've never been so pleased to leave a property as I am this one.

I get to the gate and wait for it to open.

It doesn't budge.

I flick my eyes up to my rear-view mirror. The door was closed behind me. There's nothing. There's no sign of Hester or Michelle. They aren't running out to apprehend me. The gate must be stuck, or just slow.

Patience, Jude. Patience.

My hands are sticky on the steering wheel. I can see the faintest beads of sweat beginning to form on my forehead.

I'm starting to get a bad feeling about this.

My heart almost flies up through my throat when I hear a sharp triple tap on the side window.

It's Hester.

And she doesn't look happy.

She's mouthing words I can't hear through the glass and waving at me to wind my window down.

I take a deep breath, shoot my reflection a quick look, trying to make sure I'm not showing the panic that I'm feeling, and I push the button to open the window.

"Hey," Hester says. "Why don't you step out of the car and come back to the house with me?"

I throw her my best smile.

"What's wrong?" I ask, as I try to keep the quiver out of my voice. "Did I forget something?"

"Not exactly," Hester smiles. "I didn't think you'd actually get in your car. I really thought..." She lets the sentence tail off and shakes her head.

Hester knows why I came here.

She must know.

And if Hester does, I can be almost certain that Michelle does, too.

My mind is racing, but I return the smile and reach down to switch off the engine and pull the keys from the ignition. Thinking quickly still isn't helping me to come up with any ideas of how to get out of this.

The gate is the only way forwards and out of here. I can't get through it, and there's no chance that I can climb over it. Not without Hester catching me, or without slipping and injuring myself in the process.

There's no option other than to do as she asks.

I step out of the car and join Hester on the gravel.

"Bring your bag," she gestures to the passenger seat.

"I can't stay long," I say, trying to play the innocent, just on the off chance that I'm mis-reading the situation.

I know I'm not though; I really know that I'm not.

THIRTY-NINE

Hester's smile becomes tight-lipped, and she makes a low humming sound. The kind of hum that I recognise as meaning '*we'll see about that*'.

If I grab my bag and run, can I get past her, run around the house, hide somewhere until...until what? There really are no options here. I have to go with her.

I'm screwed.

Hester is a fast walker, and my stumpy legs move in double time, trying to keep up with her as she leads me back to the house.

My car is parked there in front of the gate, making it impossible for anyone else to come or go. If either of them has called the police, the cops are going to have trouble getting past. I should be thinking about what I'm going to say to Michelle, and how I'm going to explain why I came here, and instead I'm wondering how the police are going to arrive to arrest me.

My bag feels heavier this time, on the way back to the house.

I'm still wondering if I can make a run for it, and Hester must know it, because she turns to me and shakes her head. She doesn't seem to have much to say to me, and for that I'm grateful, because I have absolutely no idea what to say to her.

Neither of them would understand why I misled them. Neither knows what was at stake for me.

I can't tell them. And even if I did, would it be a justification?

Was Hester really on to me all along? And if so, why did she leave me in the house on my own? She came over to check up on me, and surely, she couldn't have been reassured by my excuses about running away from a crappy relationship. So…what…? She told Michelle about her concerns, and they wanted to give me a chance to come clean? Or…?

I have so many questions, and I think I'm about to get some answers. But first I might have to give some.

Before we enter the house, though, Hester pulls me up.

"So, tell me. What exactly is it you were planning on doing with Michelle's documents?"

It seems that Crane has left it to her loyal servant to lead the investigation. Hester obviously knows enough to condemn me, so playing the innocent seems pointless. Taking a deep breath, I look her in the eye.

Play it cool or try to blag it? There's only a split second in which I can make my decision.

Opening my mouth, a thought suddenly occurs to me.

"Have you told her?" I ask.

Why would Michelle send Hester to bring me back to the house and get her to speak to me out here, rather than confront me herself, or, more significantly, call the police? Michelle entrusted me with her home for the three days that I've been here. If now she has realised that she might have made a huge mistake, surely she wouldn't be in the lounge relaxing. She'd be checking what else I'd taken. If I were in her position, I would be livid. There's no way that I'd be able to leave the confrontation to someone else.

"You haven't told Michelle what you *think* I've done," I say. "Why don't you explain that to me?"

"I wanted to give you the chance to explain yourself to me first," she says. I'm not buying it.

"You've worked with Ms Crane for how long? How many years? Don't you think you should be telling her what a sneaky little thief I am? If that's what you think is going on here. Shouldn't you be on the phone with the police by now?"

"The thing is, Jude, a woman like you who happens to have a perfect prior record doesn't just break bad and start stealing. You have no incentive to do this. You're paid well for your job, you get to choose your placements, someone as highly regarded as you are, and you clearly have your pick of the crop, seeing as you ended up here." Hester folds her arms and leans back against the column.

Of course, she's right.

"So…it's time to come clean. What else have you taken?" Hester asks. "Put your bag on here and unzip it." She pats the wall beside the house, indicating where she wants me to place it. "Now."

"Where's your boss?"

"Just do it," she says.

We lock eyes, and I hoist up my hold-all.

"You want to tell me what's going on?"

Hester huffs a sharp laugh.

"*Me* tell *you* what's going on? You turn up here with your shiny references and spotless record, well recommended, and obviously well connected to have landed this placement…" She shakes her head as she speaks as though she is deeply disappointed in me. The gesture reminds me of the way that Neil used to look at me, and the sickness in my gut deepens.

Hester pulls the bag across towards her and yanks it open, too impatient to wait for me to fulfil that part of her command. "…and you steal from Michelle. Just like that. No shame at all." She looks back towards me, and asks, "Why?"

I look her dead in the eye.

"I don't know what you think you know, Hester, but you're wrong. There's nothing in there apart from my make-up and laundry."

And as she searches through the bag, that's all she finds.

There are no identity documents, there's no contract, no paper at all.

Hester looks up at me with a glare of frustration, and all I can give her in return is a smug smile.

"You..." She shakes her head again in disbelief.

"I wish I..." I start to speak, but my sentence is cut short as the front doors open and Michelle Crane stands between them.

"Oh my," she says. "I think we need to talk, Jude dear. Or shall I call you Libby?"

FORTY

I haven't been known as Libby Halstead since I left my marital home three years ago. I took nothing with me. No belongings, no self-worth. All I had was my name and the measly amount of money that I'd managed to save up, - and that didn't last for long.

Hearing that word, *Libby*, the name that used to be mine, freezes me on the spot. It's almost as though my heart has stopped beating; a tight, vice-like grip embraces my entire body. I don't want to face Michelle, but I know that I have to.

"You're quite the mystery, aren't you, Jude Quinn?" Michelle asks, walking towards where Hester and I are standing.

Hester's mouth is agape, trying to take in what's happening. I can almost hear her connecting the dots in her head.

I don't like the way Michelle's looking at me, and I like it even less when she speaks again.

"Or should I say Libby Halstead?"

She knows who I am. She must know everything about me. Everything.

Did my caller tell her? When I didn't answer whatever phone calls they tried to make to me overnight, did they tip Michelle off about what I was doing here? Or at least what they thought I was doing?

There's no chance of me keeping my poker face; my calm exterior cracks down the middle, and all I can do is raise my eyes to meet hers.

"We could go with your screen name instead, if you prefer."

Michelle's expression is deadpan as she speaks the words.

"How…?" I shake my head.

I have so many questions. I don't know where to start.

"I'm sorry," I begin. "You have to understand that I would never do any of this if..." I shake my head. "You already know who I am. You know what I have to hide."

"I know," Michelle says. "I know everything."

Hester turns her gaze from me to Michelle, and then back towards me again.

"I don't know anything," she says. "Perhaps one of you could fill me in?"

I thought Hester was onto me, but hearing Michelle speaking the name I have tried to leave in my past, I realise how wrong I've been.

"Our dear Jude here isn't exactly who she claims to be," Michelle says. She walks over and positions herself beside us, so we are in a near perfect triangle formation. "As far as I can tell, the whole *Homesitters* thing is legitimate, but there's a, I won't say sordid - how about dark? - side to her past."

Hester frowns. "I tried to find out more about her. There's nothing on the internet."

"Not about Judith Quinn, no. But then again, Judith Quinn is a product of your imagination, isn't she, Libby?"

There are things I could say about Michelle. I could spill the details about the contract, the deception, the things that Michelle has done. I could tell her how I decided I was going to keep her secrets safe.

I made the wrong decision.

She knows all about me, and now I am screwed.

"I'm sorry," I say, rather than striking back. "But when...when did you know? Did they...?"

"I didn't trust her," Hester bursts in. "I was sure she was stealing from you. I checked her bag..."

"But you didn't find anything," I spit back.

"You should have come to me first," Michelle says, directing her words at Hester. "If you thought there was something suspicious. Shouldn't you have come to me?"

"I didn't want to disturb you. I thought I could handle it."

Michelle makes a low humming noise and doesn't reply. Instead, she turns to me and says, "Why don't you tell us both, then? What were you doing here?"

"House-sitting," I say. "You said so yourself. I'm a house sitter, genuinely I am. The fact that I changed my name doesn't..."

Michelle shakes her head and raises a hand to stop me from speaking.

"I know what you did when you were Libby Halstead. I know why you changed your name.

Hester looks between the two of us again.

"I was a webcam stripper," I say with resignation. There's no point hiding now.

Michelle shrugs, but Hester looks aghast.

"A little more than just a stripper, as it turns out, hmm?" I can feel the heat in my face as I think about how far out of control my life spiralled. I thought I could keep my underwear on. I thought the men would be happy to watch me dance and talk to them. Turns out if you want to make money, if you want to compete with the countless other girls doing the same thing to get by, you have to give more.

And more.

And more.

And when you're doing that, someone can take screenshots that can come back to destroy your reputation.

Who would want a house sitter than had the kind of past I have?

Michelle shakes her head.

"We both sell ourselves in one way or another," she says, almost sympathetically. It's not the reaction I had expected.

Hester remains in stunned silence.

"Come inside, Jude," Michelle says. "We need to talk."

She steps aside and gestures towards the house.

"You too, Hester. Come on."

FORTY-ONE

Michelle sits on the velvet sofa and waves towards the seat opposite.

She appears incredibly relaxed, considering. There's something zen about her entire persona though; perhaps it's related to the citrus aroma of her perfume that's wafting across to me, giving an inappropriately light feeling to this dark situation.

"Please," she says.

I don't know what's going to happen next, but I know I have no choice but to follow her directions.

As I move to the other sofa, I see something on the table that tells me she knows a lot more about what I have been doing here.

She knows about my search for the documents. She knows I found the contract. If she didn't know where it was before, she does now.

Michelle sees me looking at the object, and smiles.

She picks up the origami crane and holds it on her palm.

"You've seen this before, haven't you?" she says.

As she speaks, she pulls gently on the crane's tail, opening up the paper that it is made from, exposing the words within.

I nod. I don't know what to say.

The contract was concealed in what should have been the most obvious place. The origami crane that I found in the desk drawer in the first hour of my search was constructed from the folded document. Michelle had shown me how to open that drawer when she gave me the tour of the house. When I sat and thought about it, it was the most obvious place that I could have imagined looking.

Hidden in plain sight.

Look closely.

That's what the caller said to me.

Michelle reaches into her pocket and pulls out a shiny silver object. It's only when she holds it in her hand, flicks the lid and ignites a flame that I realise it's a lighter.

She moves the flickering blaze towards the crane's head and touches it gently, like a kiss.

"When you have a secret, you're vulnerable," she says.

The paper bird, along with the secret kept inside it, catches fire, and Michelle drops it into a wooden bowl on the table. Within a minute, there's nothing left but ash.

"When you're successful, you're vulnerable," she says, looking me dead in the eye. "I had to be sure. I had to know that my secrets were safe here." She tilts her head and pauses for a few seconds before continuing. "I told you that you were my security system, do you remember?"

I do. At the time I felt sorry for her. I couldn't help thinking how ironic it was that she thought I was her security when I was here to steal her documents. But the more she talks, the more it becomes clear that Michelle Crane has had the upper hand all along.

"Jude, dear," she says. "Your secrets are safe."

I catch my breath as the truth sinks in.

Hester can only watch as Michelle and I exchange a look of recognition.

My caller was Michelle.

It has always been Michelle.

It has always been a game.

"How could you…? Why would you…?" I don't even know what I want to ask.

"I need someone that I can trust," she shrugs, as though putting me through the past few weeks of stress and trauma is completely acceptable. "I have Hester here, but she doesn't want to do all the things that I need to ask of her."

I wonder for a moment why Michelle chose Hester as her PA if she doesn't fulfil all the criteria that Michelle requires. Michelle must have pre-empted this thought, as she continues to speak.

"Hester has been with me from the start. We've worked closely together for years."

"The contract…?" I say, and then realise my mistake before I finish the sentence.

"The contract was never real. Paper Crane is entirely my baby. If you hadn't found the documents so early, I'd never have even asked you to look for it. It was a backup to keep you busy." Michelle jerks her head with a gleeful laugh, but I'm finding it difficult to see the funny side.

"Keep me busy?" I ask.

"Entertain you. Give you something to do," she smiles. "Once you'd found the other things."

"But…" My anger is building and even though I'm trying to keep it under control, some of it slips through in my words. "Why did you do this to me? Why…?"

Michelle frowns, as though she doesn't understand.

"Do *what* to you?"

"Threaten me. Blackmail me. Put me through all that stress."

Michelle looks visibly distressed by my words.

Hester glances over at her and sighs. "A selection process," she says, slowly. "Michelle needs a stand in for the jobs I won't do. Just like she said. She was trialling you for the job."

"I didn't apply for any job. I'm a house sitter. I love what I do. I didn't need you to come along and dig up my past and…taunt me with it. I made mistakes, and I moved on. All I want is to forget the things I did." By the time I've finished speaking, tears are streaming down my face. It's the anger and frustration that's forcing them out of me.

Michelle shakes her head.

"I know who you were and what you have done. I know you were a specialist before you ran away. Before you had to make tough decisions. You were one of the best strategists in the country."

"I was a project manager."

"You were at the top of your game, and you had to give it up."

She hasn't mentioned Neil, and I don't want her to. It's bad enough that Hester knows I took my clothes off for money. She doesn't have to hear about how I let a man abuse me for so long before I had the balls to escape.

My eyes widen as that thought sinks in.

Am I really more ashamed of what he did to me than I am about my own choices?

It wasn't my fault.

I didn't deserve it.

I'm free.

I look up at Michelle.

"I got away from him," I said.

Michelle nods, wordlessly.

"I left him, and I rebuilt my life."

This time, she gives me a tight-lipped smile and holds her arms out.

Despite everything, the manipulation, the lies, the games, I lean across, and I accept the embrace. She's using my weakness as a weapon, and I realise it as her warmth presses against me. That sweet orange fragrance hits the back of my throat and as I pull back away from Michelle, I stifle a cough.

I don't need her comfort.

I withdraw to the sofa and straighten out my dress, as though brushing away the traces of Michelle's hug.

She doesn't seem fazed by this, and keeps talking.

"I was looking for a regular person with astonishing skills. Someone mentioned the name 'Libby Halstead'. And then someone else recommended her. Then another person. But Libby Halstead appeared to no longer exist." Michelle waves her hands as though showing a puff of smoke. "There were no death records, and yes, I checked, so I knew Libby must be somewhere. I just had to find her."

Michelle tilts her head to look at me.

"And of course, I found more than I expected."

"But I covered my tracks," I say. "How did you find me? Neil never found me."

Michelle looks sad for a moment. "He didn't look very hard then," she says. "I'm sorry, Jude."

He gave up on me?

Good.

Good.

I fought hard for my freedom, from that abusive relationship, and then from the hard decisions that I was forced to make in order to survive. If Neil never looked for me, there's no place in my heart for sadness. He didn't care. He never cared.

Michelle Crane, a successful, amazingly successful, business owner, an internationally renowned personality, a woman with everything to lose, put me through this. Not just this weekend that I've been here searching through her house, but the weeks before, the stress of knowing what I had to do. The fear of my darkest secrets being exposed.

I can hardly bring myself to look at her.

"I wanted you to know that you are safe here. I wanted you to know that whatever you have done in your past, you can move on from it." Michelle's voice hangs in the air.

I sit in silence, trying to focus my thoughts.

Eventually, I speak.

"I have moved on. I'm a house sitter. I'm not a project manager anymore. I'm not Libby Halstead. I'm not stuck in a relationship that terrifies me and defines every second of my life. I left that behind me, and you… what you are doing here… it's almost as bad." I pause again. "It's just as bad. This is control." I bring my eyes up to look at her. "You have manipulated me, just like he used to. This was all a game to you. Everything you said to me. Everything you did."

"You don't need to hide. You don't need to be a house sitter. You can work for me. You can…"

Every word she speaks makes the fire inside of me burn stronger.

"I'm sure most people would be grateful, Michelle," I say, cutting her off. "But I'm not most people. I'm Jude Quinn and whatever I have done, whatever I do, they're my own decisions. This," I wave my arm in a gesture around the room, "is your world. You've built yourself a beautiful life, but it's not for me. I don't want money, fame, empty bedrooms that I don't even bother to furnish because I'm so, so alone." I bite the words back, but they have already fallen from my mouth, and I finally look at Michelle to see her crestfallen reaction.

"Jude…" Hester interrupts, but seemingly can't think of the right words to say.

"Thank you," I say. "For thinking of me. For offering me this *opportunity*." I pronounce the last word with bitter sarcasm. "If you want to reveal what you know about me now, go ahead. I don't care anymore. I've rebuilt my life before, I'll do it again. Want to tell Neil where I am? He doesn't care. He just doesn't care. You don't have any power over me. I won't let you. I won't let you."

Before I can stop myself, hot tears are streaming down my face.

"Jeez, Michelle," Hester says, coming over to sit beside me and thrusting her arm towards me for a hug that this time I refuse.

"I don't need you," I tell her, looking her straight in the eyes. "I don't need either of you."

FORTY-TWO

Despite the burning anger that is raging through me, even as I speak to Hester I'm already starting to realise that there's something else. There's another wave of emotion flooding through my body: relief. I have been a slave to my secrets for so long. Ever since I left Neil. Ever since I signed up to that website and stripped for strangers. I've spent years filled with shame and guilt – but now all of those feelings are washing away.

I can't forgive Michelle for treating me as a pawn in her game, but as the realisation sinks in that maybe, just maybe, something good can come out of this, I turn to face her.

"I only wanted…" she starts talking, but I don't want to hear it. If I was interested in her words, I could read them on the internet. I don't need anything from her.

"It doesn't matter," I say. "Do what you're going to do. Ruin my reputation. Whatever." I can hardly believe that it is my voice speaking the words. "Do it."

Michelle slowly shakes her head. "I knew you might say no. I hoped, I hoped so hard that you would join me, join us, but this life isn't for everyone." She leans back, again surprisingly relaxed given the circumstances. "You could just as easily tell people what happened here. When you walk out that door, you could be on the phone to the press, telling them what I have done. You could post about me on the social media that you know I rely on for *my* reputation."

"What makes you think I won't?" I ask, my voice unwavering despite the emotional wave rushing through me.

Michelle tilts her head. "You know how important reputation is. You know what I have to lose. Even if you don't care about your own secrets anymore. I believe you. I believe that you have the power to move on, whatever happens. Even if I don't have any control over you, I think you're a good person, Jude. No matter what has happened here, you're not going to tell anyone."

I look from Michelle to Hester. She's been with Michelle how long? I can't help but wonder what the two of them know about each other, what hold Michelle has over her. This is a toxic environment, no matter how glamourous and stylish it appears on the surface.

"And Hester isn't going to say anything either," Michelle says.

Hester raises her eyebrows in a rapid flick, and nods, wordless.

"So, if I say no, and to be clear I am saying no, I can walk out of the door, and nothing will happen to me. No retribution, no looking over my shoulder, wondering when my life is going to crash around me?" I ask.

"You go with your secrets. I stay with mine." Michelle speaks the words as though what she is saying is the easiest thing imaginable.

I look at her for a moment, taking in her flawless tanned skin, soft, sheer blonde hair, the immaculate outfit that compliments her tone and figure to perfection. Michelle is an extension of this caramel cream coloured house. Sleek and stylish, but without a soul. I can't help but think about the blank rooms upstairs: empty and lonely.

Whatever this life is that Michelle has, I don't want to be part of it.

Slowly but purposefully, I rise to my feet.

"Thank you," I say. Thank you. Not for the games, but for the consequence. Not the actions, but the end result. As I walk towards the door, my feet padding one last time over the marble floor, I feel a sense of freedom that I thought I had long lost.

Whatever happens to me, I am in control.

Whatever I have done, I did because I had to.

I am Jude Quinn, and my life is finally my own.

FORTY-THREE

My flat feels different, somehow, as I settle back in. The single bedroom and compact living area are nothing compared to the sprawling square footage of Michelle's home. But every inch of this space is filled with things that I bought for myself. I have earned everything I own. This is my world. The smell of ginger and garlic intertwined with faint whispers of star anise and cinnamon rises from the Chinese restaurant below. For once, I don't mind it at all.

Once I've thrown the contents of my travel bag into the washing machine, I strip, this time for my eyes only, and for the sole purpose of jumping into my shower. Instead of the deep tub and walk-in shower cubicle of Michelle's en suite, I have a wobbly fixture that runs cold if I stand beneath it for over five minutes. I've learnt to time it. I know every detail of my own little world.

As I'm squeezing a dollop of store brand conditioner onto my hand, I hear my phone ringing where I left it in the bedroom. An instinctive rush of adrenaline jolts through me. I'm so used to hearing the voice of my caller – the disguised words of Michelle Crane – that the sound of my ringtone is enough to set my heart racing.

I fight the urge to leap out, to check it isn't her, and instead I smear the conditioner through my hair.

It's over, I tell myself. *All of it.*

The phone rings off as I rinse and use my sponge to foam Imperial Leather over my body. The smell is familiar, creamy, and sweet. Not the high-end luxury of bathing at Michelle's house, but the comforting known aroma of home.

Before the five minutes are up, I'm stepping out, drying off and wrapping myself in a slightly faded, frayed towel. I use another to form a haphazard, glamourless turban.

It's over.

I think the words again, as I fight the urge to go straight into my bedroom and retrieve the phone.

I don't have to jump when I'm told anymore. I can leave my phone. I don't need to check my messages. I…

I can't stop myself.

As much as I want to go through to the living room, switch on TV and ignore the call, I can't. I have to be sure. I have to know it's not her.

The screen tells me that there's one missed call and one voicemail.

It's not her number. It's not Michelle.

I lift the phone to my ear and listen to the message.

"Hi Jude, Penny from *Homesitters* here. Just wanted you to know that Michelle Crane has been onto the site and left a wonderful review for you. I knew you could handle it. Listen, you're not going to believe this, but Hayley Brock, the actual actress Hayley Brock, called up and asked for you personally. She's going to be away for a week and…"

I end the call before I can hear the details about the luxury house and the perfect life that Hayley lives within it. There will be other jobs. Houses with cats that like to shelter from the rain, flats with temperamental showers, nice normal homes where nice normal people live.

I'm good at what I do. Always have been, no matter what I've turned my hand to. Most of all, I'm good at being me. Libby Halstead, Jude Quinn, whatever name I go by, I'm the same person inside. Flawed. Human.

I throw my phone onto the bed, leaving the message unanswered.

Thank you for reading **The House Sitter**.

If you have enjoyed this book, please visit Amazon, Goodreads or wherever you leave reviews. Reviews help readers to find my books and help me reach new readers.

If you're posting about this book on social media, I'm @jerowneywriter, or @jerowney on TikTok. Tag me!

For further information about me and my work, and to receive a free book, please visit my website: http://jerowney.com/about-je-rowney

Best wishes,

JE Rowney

Made in the USA
Monee, IL
30 March 2024

56109496R00173